APOLLO IS MINE

GODS AND MONSTERS

MILA YOUNG

For more information, contact Mila Young.

milayoungauthor@gmail.com

Cover designer: Cover art by Cover Reveal Designs

ISBN: 978-1728685663

DEDICATION

To all my fans who have been with me from my first book.

GODS AND MONSTERS

BY MILA YOUNG

Apollo Is Mine
Poseidon Is Mine
Ares Is Mine
Hades Is Mine

APOLLO IS MINE

"When I'm with you, I feel like I've found myself," Elyse said. "And I want more."

My emotions exactly.

I climbed onto the bed and straddled her, my legs on either side of her waist, pinning her down. She ran her hands up and down my thighs.

I reached for her braid and pulled the elastic free. Dark strands spread on the bed around her like a halo. She continued to run her hands up and down my legs, inching closer and closer to my groin.

"You'll be the end of me," I growled, then dove to her mouth again, sliding my tongue between her lips, tasting her, letting myself drown. This was what I'd missed for all these years...the connection a kiss brought. Her groans. The wickedness of her tongue teasing mine.

CHAPTER 1

Elyse

I spun and kicked back, aiming for the solar plexus. Heracles stepped out of the way, and with lightning speed, he was behind me, his arm around my neck. He squeezed until I couldn't breathe, my lungs stinging. Panic swirled in my gut.

I grabbed his arm with both hands and pulled down, curling my body into a ball. It threw him off-balance, enough for me to get out of his death grip and gasp for air. He redeemed himself in no time—he was a demigod, after all, and he didn't fall for the primitive moves of a mere human. I felt his power push down on me like a giant hand—not his physical strength, but the magic that came with his god side. It made it harder to focus as his magic gave off electrical sparks against my very essence.

But I wasn't fully human either. Once I harnessed the strength of the gods in me, I could hold my own in a fight. Most of the time. I reached deep and tugged at that line inside me that plugged me into Zeus directly. Yes, the king of the gods. The magic simmered beneath my skin like fire, and I pushed the invisible power at Heracles, slamming into him.

Eyes wide open, he staggered on the spot. Our energies crashed into each other, sending out a wave that knocked over the chairs in the corner of the empty Chicago community hall we fought in and sent them sprawling.

I used Heracles's arm, which I still held on to, and swung around, heaving myself up to land on his back, wrapping my legs around his torso as best I could. One arm was around his mouth and nose, the other around his throat. I had him.

Heracles didn't agree. Grunting, he fell backward, using his weight to pin me, and it forced all the air out of my lungs. I didn't let go of my grip, but Heracles had the upper hand now. Damn him. He rolled over, and somehow, his hands were on my shoulders, his knees on my legs, and I could do nothing but stare at his smirk.

"You're dead," he said in a low voice.

I groaned and squeezed my eyes shut. "I have more lives."

"Not infinite. You only have three. Don't waste them," he snarled.

Why had Zeus given my family a limit on how many lives we had while we fought gods and creatures that were close to impossible to defeat? My ancestors had been fighting evil on Earth for so long, no one remembered exactly how long ago Zeus had blessed us. While we were strong and had supernatural abilities, we could still die from injuries like normal humans, and then we awoke in the same body, age, and time we died... basically we'd survived death. But if we were lucky enough to die of natural old age, the catch was, we were dead forever. No being reborn with another life. Zeus had a funny sense of humor, apparently.

"That's not fair." I wriggled for release.

"It's never fair in the field. Do you think it was fair when I faced my twelve labors? No, but I overcame my fear and succeeded." He raised his chin in pride like he always did when he spoke of his achievements. Those sharp cheekbones gave him a chiseled look, and there was no denying he was handsome. But the demigod sure loved to brag.

"Elyse, you're smaller than I am in size," he continued. "You're smaller than any of the creatures or gods you're battling. So you have to fight smart," he insisted.

"Let me up," I rumbled.

Heracles released me, and I rolled over, panting. I hated whenever I lost to him during our training sessions. Which was often, considering he was powerful enough to take down gods. I hated the way he tried to hold back the grin each time. I hated that I still hadn't mastered my strength.

"I can't do this, Herc," I responded. "You're only a demigod, and I can't even beat you. What happens when my opponents are all magic without an ounce of humanity?"

Heracles frowned. "Thanks for that," he said sarcastically, shadows crowding under his eyes. "But I can take on any god, so if you beat me, you'll be ready to go."

"I didn't mean it that way. But our powers are more evenly matched. The other gods are bound to be stronger, right?" I had battled monsters before, but never a hostile god who intended to harm humans.

Heracles sighed loudly, running a hand through his sandy hair. "You can do this. My dad didn't choose your family for this task because he thought any of you were weak."

I shook my head. "Strength in numbers, remember? And where are those numbers? I'm the only one left." My voice climbed as my stomach hardened at the injustice of my family line appointed to protect humans from godly monsters, yet we weren't given the same abilities to battle them adequately. So everyone I loved had been killed in battle. I glanced down, blinking to push back the tears, reminding myself to slow my breaths. This wasn't Heracles's fault. He was the only one helping me.

My phone buzzed from inside my bag against the wall. I ignored it as Heracles kneeled in front of me where I sat on the foam mat. His eyes were cerulean blue, set in that Greek face of his. His nose was long and straight, his brows low, and he had the classic Greek olive skin that made everyone do a double-take. The humans knew Heracles was something else, but they could never put their fingers on it. It wasn't that he was built like an Adonis himself or he had eyes that made you shiver to your core. The gods all had something about them that made the humans fear them yet adore them at the same time.

Wasn't like I was in that category at all. Not even the slightest. I certainly didn't adore the gods. More like I had a love-hate thing going on with them. And the feeling was mutual at best. Zeus had given my family bloodline the power that ran through our veins as a birthright for generations. I was born of a lineage that had been chosen to fight the "Good Fight" here on Earth while these gods were busy with more important things on Mount Olympus. I snorted a laugh. Yeah right. But I was one of them, in a way.

"You've come a long way," Heracles stated, his voice sharp and authoritative. "Your father would be proud."

At the mention of my dad, a pang of sorrow shot into my chest. His death had been the most recent, and the open wound still smarted, burrowing deep. That hollowness reminded me how alone I was in the world. But I pushed the agony away. I couldn't let the tragedy that had haunted my family for centuries distract me while we trained. I didn't want Heracles to know it was a weakness. My father's death had left me with no one, and I was terrified of dying for real.

Didn't matter that I could come back three times before it was my final death. Yep, logic made no sense when it came to fear. It just bubbled in my chest like a bomb about to detonate each time I imagined myself dying. Maybe I'd seen too many people I loved lose their lives too soon…I don't know. But I wasn't ready to leave this world.

"I realize I'm better than I was, but do you think it's enough?" I stared into the bluest eyes for any sign of what he really thought.

Heracles folded his massive limbs until he was crosslegged like me. Somehow, it looked wrong. That formidable body in shorts and T-shirt was made for battle, not hanging out on the floor.

"It's only enough if you believe it is."

Right. It was all in my head. He reminded me of that all the time. And I felt good about myself when I fought. Most of the time, I could ignore the nagging fear that I wasn't good enough and drag out the ability that made me stronger, faster, more powerful than other humans.

"Let's stretch," he suggested.

I rolled my eyes, huffing. "I'm tired."

"You'll be sore tomorrow if you don't stretch. This is training one-oh-one. Don't be a baby." He brushed his light brown hair backward over his temples, looking like he'd just stepped out of a hairdresser, while I sweated.

I groaned.

He burst out in laughter, the sound savage and echoing around us. "Always the dramatic one."

I fake-punched him in the arm. "You can't talk."

When he cocked a brow, I climbed to my feet. "Let's get this over with."

When our training session ended, Heracles picked up his duffle bag and turned toward me with a smile. "Good session. See you first thing in the morning?"

After I nodded, he left the training center to head home. Heracles lived on Earth, even though he had earned his way back into Mount Olympus centuries ago. He preferred staying with the humans, seeing that his adoptive parents and his true love, Megara, had been human. It had all been so long ago, it was purely a myth to everyone now. But to Heracles, Earth felt like home, he'd once told me. To the point where he taught self-defense classes at the local gymnasium, became an adventure junkie, and even had a profile on Tinder. Not that he needed to, but he insisted on keeping his options open until he found someone he clicked with. Mind you, he'd been on over a hundred dates with women who fawned over him, yet he still turned them down. Personally, I didn't believe he was over Megara, and he searched for an elusive replacement who didn't exist.

We'd been training every day of the week and on the weekend for the past five months. Since losing my dad, I took this a lot more seriously and wished I had done so when he'd been alive.

For now, every day was the same. No breaks. I only kept track of the days because of my friend. And he helped me not just because of the promise to his dad but to ensure we had a fighting chance to protect innocents.

His routine was the same as mine. Or maybe mine was the same as his. He was always around to help me.

I climbed into my SUV and threw my gym bag onto the back seat. It landed next to the camera bag I always carried with me. I stared at the concrete community hall Heracles hired for a couple of hours every day. There were bars on the windows and weeds growing across the front yard, but this place offered the people a place of hope. Locals could hire it for boxing classes for kids, gymnastics, and yoga.

My legs were numb, and my heart rate was still elevated despite the cool-down session we'd had. My chest hurt, but that wasn't from fighting.

Heracles had brought up my dad because he'd wanted me

to know that Ernest Lowe would have been proud of his only surviving child. But I wished he hadn't brought it up.

Dad had died a hundred and eighty-three days ago. His death was still fresh in my mind. My brothers had already been gone by then. My dad had fought the Aeternae near an old abandoned hospital alone, and they had gotten the better of him, taking his last life.

I hated Zeus for that. When Zeus had given us our power, given the Lowe family and all their descendants the ability to protect the Earth from Death, some gods had countered our attacks by sending us mythical creatures to battle. If we didn't, they would kill the humans, and the more souls Hades could gather, the more Death won out.

My father had told me about Death when I'd been a little girl. I used to sit around the table with my brothers, and my father would tell us about a being that was unlike anything else. He lived with Hades, almost as a second personality in his very skin, and to those who knew him, Death was merely known as X. He had a name, but to mention it was to summon him, and no one wanted to die before their time.

X was the one who'd sent the Aeternae, the Griffins, the Centaurs, and the Chimera for us to fight when he figured we were bored. Or when he was.

The Aeternae were rhino-like creatures with sawtooth bones on their heads with which they maimed and killed.

My father had been powerful. He had been one of the strongest Lowes in existence, but it had been a case of numbers. There'd been too many Aeternae, and my mother and brothers had already long been dead. Anyone who married into the Lowe family, didn't get the three-life gift. It was a blessing passed down through blood.

I had been away for photography work in Fresno, real work, not just a cover. I still blamed myself for not being there to help him fight, no matter how much Heracles told me it wasn't my fault.

X hadn't been the one to take my father's soul when he'd died. None of us would belong to Hades once our time was up. When we died, we were taken to live with the other heroes of old in peace. It was the only thing that made my father's death a little more bearable, but the whole absolute of leaving behind Earth and everyone I knew terrified me.

Anyway, X hadn't been able to get his stinking fingers on my father's soul, and he didn't swim eternally in the River of Souls that Hades watched over in the Underworld. My family—all of them—were at peace.

So now I trained alone here on Earth, my only confidant and companion the demigod Zeus had appointed to train the Lowes, his task on Earth that would justify him not returning to Mount Olympus. Heracles had become a shoulder to cry on, a grief counselor after my father's death, and a friend. And I trained because it was in my blood and so my dad's death hadn't been in vain. I'd carry on what he'd died for.

My phone beeped again. I grabbed it from my gym bag and found a message from a client buying several of my photographs I'd taken of an old, torn-down building. Fantastic, it meant money to pay my rent. I backed the car out of the parking lot and drove to my apartment on a busy street with cars parked in every spot along the curb. Luckily, I had reserved parking at the back of the building. There were no trees or shrubs on the sidewalk here. Only cement and concrete.

The sky was gray and lightning played across the heavens, but it wasn't going to rain, according to my weather app. There'd been a time when I remembered the world to be a sunnier place, but Chicago was mostly cloudy now. The sun barely made an appearance. They blamed it on global warming. I wasn't so sure it was that simple.

At home, I undid the long braid I always wore my hair in, stripped off my training clothes—sneakers, yoga pants, and fitness tank top—and climbed into the shower. The water ran through my hair and over my body, easing my sore muscles. Every week, I was getting stronger, my body fitter and more toned than it had ever been. When I looked in the mirror, I stared at a warrior. My dark hair offset my pale skin that was typical of a Lowe, and my father's honey-colored eyes were haunted and filled with rage. He was the only reason I still did all of this. Sometimes, I believed I was a fool for still fighting.

There were Lowes spread all over the Earth, but if they hadn't been killed, they'd abandoned the cause or hadn't been taught about it at all because their forefathers had refused to support the fight. Their powers had dwindled from disuse, and I was alone still pushing on. I would avenge my family if nothing else.

If I gave up, their deaths would be for nothing.

When I climbed out of the shower, I turned on the radio in my room. All the stations were filled with talking. There was no music, only a constant chatter. Struggling to follow the conversation, I turned it back off. The silence was better.

After drying my hair, leaving it loose over my shoulders, I made a quinoa salad with raw salmon on the side. I trained hard, and I ate right. I never drank. Power like mine and losing control when I was drunk was a terrible combination. My brother Seth had proved that before he'd died.

I sat down on the couch with my meal and switched on the television.

Someone knocked on my door, and I groaned. I didn't feel like getting up; plus, I was starving.

"Elyse," Heracles called. I recognized his voice through the door. I frowned. Heracles never came to my apartment.

I pushed myself up from the couch and hurried to the front door. When I opened it, Heracles stood there larger than life, his brow furrowed with concern. He wore the leather armor he was depicted wearing in all the images in books and on the internet, complete with the rubber wristbands, the leather strip skirt, and the sandals. He held the golden shield as if it were made of paper. A black strip was tied around his forehead, and his light chestnut hair was pulled back in a ponytail of sorts. He looked divine, to say the least. I lost my breath and was pretty sure my neighbors might die of shock at seeing him dressed up this way.

"Did you go see your dad? Or are you heading to a costume party?" I teased, hoping it was the latter since that meant this wasn't a serious talk. Or maybe for a change, he was inviting me out to have fun?

He stepped into the apartment, all shoulders and brooding. Worry knotted in my gut. I'd never seen him dressed like this. Supernatural energy radiated off him like steam, and I had to take a few deep breaths to steady myself.

"What's wrong?"

He arched an eyebrow as if my comment didn't warrant a response. "Yeah, I went to see Dad, and I'm here to warn you. Something big is coming." His velvety voice was deeper than usual. The more time he spent on Earth between visits to his dad, the more the god-quality wore off and he seemed more like a human. A perfectly sculpted, crazy attractive human, but still. When he came back from Mount Olympus, he was riddled with power that skipped down his arms.

"Like what?" I asked, not sure I was ready to press the panic button yet. He had a habit of over-worrying, like last month when he'd insisted I shouldn't visit the new café in town that had a peacock for its brand. I'd seen no issue with it, while he'd insisted the location was affiliated with Hera. Oh yeah, someone still held a grudge against the Queen of the Olympian gods, who believed peacocks were sacred. Then again, Hera had tricked Heracles into going mad and he killed his loved ones. Anyway, I'd visited the café and had the best coffee ever. Plus, I'd survived.

Heracles shifted his weight from one foot to the other, as if he struggled to stand in the afterglow of the gods, just like me. It buzzed in my veins, as if I'd eaten two big chocolate blocks in a row. And now, I hummed on a high.

"I don't know." Worry marred his brow. "My father warned me. Hades is causing trouble in the Underworld. Whatever is going to happen, it will probably come up from the Underworld. You have to be ready." He spoke fast, the bridge of his nose pinching.

Suddenly, fear clutched at my throat, and my chest was tight. "What if I'm not ready? This is freaking Hades we're talking about! I can't even defeat you!"

He stiffened, squaring his shoulders. "You have to be ready, Elyse. You're the only one left, and if something is coming and you don't do anything, a lot of people are going to die." He gripped his hips, staring down at me as if I were a child in the same way my dad used to do when I'd refused to train.

I closed my eyes and forced myself to breathe. I could do this. Wasn't this what I'd been training for? Besides, I couldn't stand Hades, so whatever he sent our way deserved an ass-kicking.

But I hoped to God that Hades wasn't personally going to visit Earth. And this was why I so wished Heracles had said we were going to a costume party instead. Because if I was taking on the god of the Underworld on my own, I might as well sign my own death warrant right now.

CHAPTER 2

Elyse

I met Catina at Metric Coffee Co. as soon as she'd gotten off work. It was what they called an industrial chic café, where they sold artisan coffee. The coffee was more Catina's thing, but after Heracles's news, I'd felt the darkness creeping in, and I'd had to get out. His power stayed behind after he'd left, making it hard to catch a breath again. He provided no additional information, just that grave danger was coming.

Great. But gods and monsters didn't work on schedules—they appeared when they wanted, and anywhere. Dad had always told me not to stop my life for them. Be alert, prepared, and always ready, but don't forget to keep living. Which I was, hence my need for caffeine, and I had no doubt if Heracles heard anything more on Hades's plan, he'd let me know.

"Are you okay, Elyse?" Catina asked as we sat down at one of the few tables scattered around with our coffee.

I nodded, sipping the hazelnut espresso I'd ordered. "I'm sore from training. I had another session this morning."

"What are you working out so hard for?" Catina's voice was whiny in a cute way. "You never compete in any athletics or running marathons. Granted, you look stunning because of it."

I shrugged. "I enjoy it. You know that."

"Yeah, you've always been serious about training." She shook her head, as if unable to make sense of my obsession to keep fit, but what was I going to do, tell her the truth?

"I remember you were the only person who ran for miles before school," Catina continued. Though she riled me up about working out every time we met, I suspected she was a smidgen jealous. If I didn't have to save humanity, I'd spend more time shopping and do the things normal people did.

Catina and I had gone to the same school. I'd been lonely in a world where no one understood who I was or what burden rested on my shoulders. Catina had reached out to me. At first, I hadn't wanted to be friends with the blonde bombshell, the cheerleader with a million followers and the hottest guy on her arm. But she had insisted, making a nuisance of herself until I'd caved and started hanging out with her. She'd grown up moving a lot for her father's job, and she'd hated how hard it was to keep making new friends. When she'd seen me alone, something about me had struck a chord with her.

We'd been inseparable ever since.

Besides, I liked having a friend who wasn't involved in my chaotic mess of a life. I loathed having to lie about why I trained so hard and who my instructor was. Catina wouldn't believe me if I told her Heracles was my mentor. But I enjoyed hanging out with her because it reminded me that aside from the magic and the fighting and the deaths in my family, I was still human.

Catina talked to me about clothes and makeup. She was a columnist at *Foundation*, a women's magazine. She wrote about fickle things like, "The Perfect Shoe for Every Occasion" and "Red Lips that Scream You're Trying Too Hard." The simplicity of her life was a pleasure to listen to, and I loved it when she droned on.

I sipped my coffee and listened to what she referred to as "drama" at work, where one of her colleagues had slept with the boss's son. It sounded petty to me, but things like that just didn't feature in my life. The gods all slept with each other. The Greek deities were a horny bunch, and I had been raised with the stories of all their mortal lovers and children.

I saw sex and lovers in a different light from almost everyone else. I didn't even view love in the same way. Love was at the bottom of my priority list.

First: Save the World.

Second: Don't die more than twice.

The rules were simple.

As for sex? If I had the time and a guy that was worth a damn, why not?

After I left the coffee shop, I felt refreshed and my mind cleared to focus on Heracles's ominous warning.

I stood in front of my door looking for my keys as Oliver, my next-door neighbor, stepped out of his apartment. His easy smile welcomed me as it had my first I moved into my apartment five months ago.

"How's work?" He raked his light hair out of his eyes. His lanky frame pressed against the doorframe of his apartment. The top of his hair stuck up from his hand combing. His Hawaiian print shirt didn't distract from his handsomeness, even if it did make him come across as goofy. He worked for a marketing firm, and at twenty-four, was the youngest marketing manager at the company. At two years his junior, I had no comparable career but loved my photography hobby.

"Any new projects?" he asked.

I shook my head, shifting the camera bag strap on my shoulder. "Nah. In between gigs right now." A perfect conversation starter apparently, especially with my flirty neighbor who seemed to always bump into me in the corridor of our apartment. No coincidence there.

As a freelance photographer, I took my camera everywhere with me, and if I sold my photos to the right people, I made enough money to get by. My bookings were scattered, which freed up time for training, and I could use the job as an excuse as to why I was out of town every now and then.

Every superhero needed a cover, right? Although I wasn't exactly a hero. I fought beasts because it was in my family lineage. My calling. Since I'd lost my dad, the call had grown stronger. I yearned to show him I had no plans of letting him down.

"What are you doing this weekend?" Oliver's voice dipped as if he'd practiced for hours to get the courage and ask me.

"I have plans," I said with a smile, feeling bad to keep turning him down, but being with me would get him killed. So I kept my distance and didn't date anyone. Sure, the occasional fling had happened the couple of times Catina had insisted on dragging me out to dance clubs. But with me fighting ferocious creatures, such a lifestyle didn't lend itself to a relationship. Though Dad had found Mom, in the end, it had gotten her killed. So I'd made the decision long ago to stay single.

"Are you ever going to not have a gazillion things going on when I try to ask you on a date?" Oliver's words climbed. Clearly, he'd found his confidence. He pushed away from the doorframe, tall and serious.

I grinned politely. "I told you, Oliver. I don't go out with anyone."

He sighed. "Yeah, you said that. I was hoping you would

change your mind once you got to know me better. How will you know you don't want to be with me if you don't try?"

"It's not you. I just don't date. Nothing personal." Discomfort settled in my chest at the idea of turning him down again, but it was for his own good. In a different place and time, I'd say *yes* in a heartbeat. I couldn't even entertain the idea of placating him with going out for drinks because that would be me leading him on. I couldn't do that to him.

"Classic 'it's not you, it's me' scenario, huh?" Oliver huffed, stuffing his hands into the pockets of his jeans.

I nodded, having had this conversation many times already with Oliver and other guys, too. "I'm as cliché as they get." My laughter came out strained.

He chuckled. "There's nothing cliché about you. But all right. I'll have you know I'm not going to stop trying."

I smiled and unlocked my door, stepping into the apartment.

I felt bad for him. He was a nice guy—had always been kind to me anyway—and he wasn't unattractive at all. But I couldn't date him. He had no idea what my life was like, and somehow, I didn't think he'd be able to stomach it if he understood what I was. I doubted Oliver had a strong constitution.

My family had been given this ability ages ago, and the Lowes had married and reproduced over and over again. Somehow, though, I couldn't imagine bringing children into a world where they were likely to die before their time, and where they had to lead a double life.

I wished I could be with someone like Oliver. I wished I had a normal life where I could fuss about trivial things like clothes and makeup and I could work a career for the sake of having a career, not a front like Superman and his work as a journalist. Maybe, if I were only a human, I'd be happy with someone like Oliver.

And why not? There were plenty of Lowes all over the globe who had shucked their responsibility, and they married, had kids, and jobs like any other mortal. They were probably happy.

At least, I imagined they ought to be. I didn't know any of them personally. If I Googled "Lowe," I bet I could find them, but in our family, we shunned those who refused to embrace their destiny. I had grown up believing that abandoning the cause was a betrayal, and we turned our backs on them. Though I sympathized with their decision. Risking your life and confronting terrifying three-headed beasts wasn't everyone's cup of tea. But maybe somewhere out there was a Lowe who didn't know what they could be, and maybe I'd find someone else to fight alongside me.

Still, doing the honorable thing had been ingrained in me since I'd been a child, and my dad and my brothers still had to be avenged. So instead of defecting, I would carry on fighting for a while longer.

I plonked down in front of my laptop and hooked up my camera. Over the past few days, I'd taken numerous photos that I planned to edit before adding them to my online portfolio. Maybe I'd find another buyer or two, so I might be able to add them to my newsletter.

The recent batch were all photographs of people. I flicked through the pics one by one. I was fascinated by the people, how they moved from one task to the next in their lives, how parts of who they were showed in the way they did things, even when they weren't trying at all. Did someone look at me and see the same? Was I unique like these people, with small parts that fit together to create a bigger picture? Or was I only comprised of my mission and now also my grief?

My skin prickled, and I struggled to concentrate on the photo I was trying to edit. I felt uncomfortable. My stomach churned with something that felt like nerves, and my chest grew tighter.

I ignored the feeling and kept working. I had to take care of this, not only for my portfolio that I presented for new projects I bid on, but also for my own sanity. I kept in touch with humanity this way. It reminded me why I was doing what I was doing.

After a while, my insides started quivering. The magic inside of me pushed against my skin from my core, as if it were trying to break free. I took deep breaths, trying to contain myself, but my magic was like a beast, curled up but awake, biding its time, waiting for something.

I knew what it was waiting for, too.

Whatever Heracles had warned me about was coming closer. I could feel it. Time seemed to slow, and I was caught in a bubble. The oxygen was thin, and the walls pressed in on me.

By the time I couldn't stand it a second longer, I jumped up and changed into tracksuit pants and a tank top. I put on my running shoes, lacing them up, and dashed to the door. As soon as I was outside, the midday sun broke through the gray clouds, and I could breathe again. I sucked the air into my lungs and hiked down to the road. The Earth was alive with anticipation. It hummed under my feet softly, with the knowledge that something was arriving soon. Not yet, but soon enough. And I'd be ready.

I turned in a direction—any direction worked—and started running. My feet pounded a tattoo on the tarmac, and my muscles rejoiced at being worked again. I ran through the city, not caring about good neighborhoods or bad ones. No one was going to approach me with the power surging through me like this. They wouldn't survive doing something to me.

All I wanted was to get rid of some of the built-up tension and energy. I had to eliminate whatever it was I was feeling, and running until I couldn't run anymore usually did the trick. Shoving aside the doubts and worries, I accepted that the biggest fight of my life might be coming my way.

CHAPTER 3

Hades

Fuck love. That was all I could say. It was a shitty ride from the start, even if I'd thought I was in love. But it hadn't been real, and now that I was free of that spell, I was over the whole damn thing. Even my heart sat quietly in my chest, resolved to the fact that everything came to an end eventually.

Hera, my sister, had been a bitch. She'd had a bet going with one of the other gods—probably Eros—and Eros had won it by proving they could make even me fall in love. Because I was the black sheep of the family, right? I was the asshole who had drawn the short straw when my brothers and I had decided who was going to rule. Zeus had chosen the heavens to rule, and Poseidon had taken the seas. And me? I had received the Underworld and part of measly little Earth with mortals. Hip-fucking-hooray.

I'd had enough of being left behind, of being a joke. Things were going to change around here.

"Keep an eye on things, will you?" I commanded across the chamber to Persephone. She stood with her back to me, gazing at herself in the mirror, wearing her newest gown, this one pebbled in gold jewels. They glimmered and winked against the flames roaring in the fireplace. The fabric fell to her ankles, following the curves of her body. No denying, she was beautiful, but my heart no longer sang for her. I'd lost the spirit that had driven me to adore her. Now, I felt empty, barren, and sorrowful. Not for the loss of love, but time wasted on what I had once believed was real. How wrong I'd been.

Around the room, dried flowers in frames riddled the black walls. Gone were my statues of wolves and owls, along with the portraits of Cerberus. Fuck, the place resembled a garden party more than where the god of the Underworld lived. Even hibiscus flowers were printed on the king-sized bedspread. Persephone had insisted they made her feel close to her mother, Demeter, the goddess of Harvest and Fertility. How the hell was I supposed to fuck my love while we were surrounded by things that symbolized her mother? Yep, well, there hadn't been action in my bed for way too long.

Fire soared through my veins. Everything about my life constricted around me like a noose. Where had things gone wrong? For the past few years, during Persephone's six-month visits, she'd grown more distant, despondent, not talking to me for weeks. Instead, she'd spend her time getting the tailor to create her new gowns with the crystals the dead mined for me. Yep, we had grown apart long ago, and now I had to make a change. A reckless adrenaline ruled my actions because for too long I'd done what everyone expected of me. But I'd lost who I'd thought I loved… and now I planned to do something for myself for a change. The Underworld pretty much ran itself, anyway.

I turned to Persephone, who still stared in the mirror, lifting her long, dark locks into a curled bun on top of her head, puckering her blood-red lips in the reflection. "And let me know when the Fates need to see me."

"I can handle it," she replied blandly.

This was like a fucking custody case. The Fates—the three witches who shared one eye and one tooth among the three of them and ruled over the past, the present, and the future of the humans—used to be my responsibility. I supposed there wasn't some divine court case that would decide who got to take care of them.

Good thing I didn't give a shit about rules. Apollo had been roaming the Earth for a while, and Zeus hadn't come after him for breaking the law. He would have to leave me alone too. It was only fair.

"I'm off," I blurted out.

"Earth's not what it used to be," Persephone teased, glancing at me over her shoulder, her dark eyes glinting under the fire's flickering light. When she returned to the outside world, they morphed into a sky-blue color, and I'd once adored them, but now they held an iciness when she looked at me.

"I don't care."

She shrugged. "You will when you see it."

Persephone had been the goddess of spring. The Earth used to be her home, which it still was six months a year. For a long time, I believed she loved me back, and maybe she did in her own way, but whatever we had experienced had faded and perhaps that was because I'd forced her to stay away. Or was it her mother's influence, who knew? But things weren't working out between us, as hard as I'd tried. She was the unlucky goddess whom I'd seen first after the spell had been put on me. I'd fallen for her so fucking hard, I'd gotten a concussion, and I'd tricked her into staying with me. It was amazing what the bite of a poisonous apple could do. Or the Underworld pomegranate in this case.

It was all fine and dandy because even though she didn't love me, I had showered her with gifts until she was sure I was her Prince Charming.

The problem with buying love was that it expired. Yeah, it had taken a couple of centuries for that to happen, and it had taken another couple of centuries to finally admit it wasn't working between us. Here, we were separated like the modern humans who got married and divorced, as if they only now understood that mortals were never meant to mate for life.

Since Persephone had become the Princess of the Underworld when she'd tied herself to me—the fact that it was against her will was irrelevant—she now also had the ability to command over the souls of the dead in the underworld like I did. Which meant the Underworld was her home. I had forced her in there with that pomegranate trick that had essentially been a contract between us. So she remained the Princess of the Underworld even if I left.

I sure as fuck wouldn't cry over this. I'd spent enough years grieving for my lost love. Those days were over.

Now, I'd live among the mortals because anything was better than staring at my ex in the face every night, knowing I had simply never been good enough. Fuck that. I had been more than she deserved, but she had no clue what she now lost.

The thing that drew me to Earth more than anything else? It was loveless. Humans had changed a lot since the beginning. They fought more now, they were greedy and selfish, and love was a chore.

We agreed on the last part.

While I was with them, I would rule on a throne built by the greatness of my existence, and I would revel in the fact that love was nowhere to be found. Because who needed love? Sure as shit wasn't me.

I rode to Earth in the form of a screech owl, my sacred animal. Cool air buffeted against my golden feathers, polluted air, but still fresh air compared to the underground. When I landed on grass in a small field near skyscrapers I'd seen in magazines and television because we got cable in the Underworld, I was in my godlike form again, clothed in only the best garbs. I knelt on the ground and pushed my fingers into the soil, feeling the cold, the grittiness. It vibrated against my touch.

"Oh, you've been expecting me," I breathed. The Earth hummed in response. She was mine to control and rule, the metals and precious gems it rendered running like veins through a heart. My magic called it to life.

I stood again and took a deep breath.

Movement caught my eye, and I turned to find a figure in front of me. My heart banged, not ready to be followed onto Earth.

"Why are you here?" I demanded.

X stood next to me. He was in human form now, a figure he hadn't taken in a long time. Tall and thin with skin the color of dark chocolate, and black hair that hung around him like a cloak. His eyes were black, but when he turned toward me, they reflected red as if they were alive. You'd be surprised how much the dead complained about.

"I'm here because you're here," he replied, his voice a hiss, and I resonated with the fear that flowed from him like a fog. I breathed it in and relished it, wrapping it around myself like a second skin.

X was usually a part of me in a big way. He was Death. And I? I was the ruler of the Underworld, the god of the

Dead, and the River of Souls. But we were different entities.

"You should have stayed in the Underworld with Persephone," I growled bitterly.

X shook his head. "You set me free."

And in that instant, he disappeared as if he'd evaporated, before I could ask what the fuck he was talking about. Oh, well, good riddance. X wasn't my favorite character to hang out with. Just because he was so much a part of me didn't mean we had ever had slumber parties. X was the side of me I had always loathed. Depressing and only interested in how to collect fresh souls.

I turned back toward the city that sprawled in front of me. Chicago, they called it. Something about this place called to me. I couldn't put my finger on it, but if energy drew me, I went to it. Everything had a purpose, and I was curious what this city had in store for me.

A jagged array of buildings across the horizon. A couple strolled farther away in the park I'd arrived in, so I made my way to the nearest road to head into the city, to study the place I would lay claim over.

But it was dark, overcast everywhere in Chicago. Where the hell was the sun? Apollo had really fucked up in this city, hadn't he? Persephone had been right. Earth wasn't what it used to be.

When I had been here last, centuries ago, Earth had been warm and green and picturesque. Music and poetry and light had been everywhere. Art. Dance. The beauty of speech that bubbled from the lips of humans. Now, the world was full of darkness and hatred, with murky skies, music that was more talking than harmony, and art and dance had fallen away. The humans destroyed instead of created. Yet they told themselves they were happy.

But they were miserable. I sensed it in my veins like a

wriggling serpent. Maybe I was going to be happier than I'd thought here.

My whole body pulsated like a tuning fork. Something in the city drew me in a way I disliked.

And I knew exactly where that energy belonged.

Zeus had decided that to prevent me from wreaking havoc on the poor humans—like fucking me over hadn't been enough—he had imported some divine power onto a family that would become the supernatural guardians of the race. The Lowe family.

I had watched them train and become stronger. At first, they'd held their own. But as time had passed, they had flaked. Given up. Or died. Humans were pathetic. I didn't know why Zeus had thought it would mean something to put them in charge of their own fates. The humans were self-destructive idiots. Like dodos, they were too dumb to survive by themselves. If it weren't for the gods, they would have gone extinct ages ago.

The Lowe family had been chosen, and the power in me recognized the ability they possessed. But their energy wasn't scattered over the Earth as it once had been. It was concentrated in one place. There was only one left. Well, that was interesting.

I laughed loud and sharp, drawing the attention of the couple who strolled across the park.

"Is this the best you can do?" I shouted up at the heavens. I knew Zeus was listening. Asshole.

"Your precious humans are in for a ride," I snarled.

Thunder and lightning danced across the sky.

"If you want to play, we can play," I called out.

Zeus was taunting me with a display of authority, but I wasn't in the mood to be good. I was pissed off that I had been rejected, and I wanted to fuck around. What better place than to do it here in my new domain, where there were few rules?

A little Lowe wouldn't do anything to stop me from being here.

The sound of an engine roared through the dusky air, and I spun around. I trailed the black motorbike as it drove past, the rider's sky-blue eyes locking on mine. The bike changed direction and came back toward me.

When it stopped, Apollo put his feet on the earth and leaned an elbow on one knee. Of course, he would have sensed my arrival and come to lay down his territorial protective shit. His arms flexed, showing off the muscles in the sleeveless shirt he wore, and his golden hair hung over a shoulder.

"What the fuck are you doing here, Hades?" he growled.

"I'm doing what you're doing: whatever the fuck I want." I laughed, lifting my chin, showing him I had no plans of leaving. This was my new home.

Apollo shook his head, the bridge of his nose wrinkling, his voice lowering to a deep grumble. "I don't need trouble. There has been peace on Earth from the gods, so we don't need you stirring shit. Leave and go back to your depressing hole in the ground."

I squared my shoulders, grinning widely for show, holding Apollo's stare. "Stay out of my way, golden boy." I shrugged. "I'm not here to pick a fight with you."

"But you'll get one if you mess this up for me," Apollo hissed, his shoulders curled forward. "I've been living here for a long time. Your brother and I have a deal. If you do anything to screw that up for me, then you and I are going to have problems." He lifted his square chin, his eyes narrowing with his threat.

I rolled my eyes. "You're such a drama queen. Must be all that poetry and art bubbling out of your ass."

"Fuck you, Hades," Apollo snarled, kickstarting his bike to life. It hollered to life, and Apollo drove away. I chuckled. Apollo hated it when anyone reminded him who he was. It interfered with his badass image. Hypocrite.

But I wasn't exactly the complimenting type.

I looked around again at my world and nodded. This was going to be fun.

CHAPTER 4

Elyse

*O*n my way to the shops on this morning, a goddamn centaur ran across the road in front of my car. My heart hit the back of my throat as he galloped away, propelling forward, a thundering of hooves resonating in his wake. Muscles rippled from under his chestnut pelt and powerful legs, black hair flowing wildly over his powerful shoulders and back.

I slammed on my brakes, not to swerve out of the way, but to get out and fight the damn thing. Behind me, a car's tires screeched at my sudden halt, so I swung over to the curb. No one on the sidewalk or in traffic panicked because humans couldn't see the creature. Centaurs were invisible to humans. All creatures were.

I'd hoped for a relaxing day at the mall, but the Lowes never got a day off. My dad had taught me that at a young age, and it was true as I rarely spent days with my friends and watching TV growing up. I'd always get called to attend urgent missions, like the time we'd had to capture and contain a chimera.

I put on my hazards and locked my car before setting off after the beast. A centaur had the torso of a man and the body of a horse, so with four legs, it could outrun me. But it wouldn't. They were just another of the creatures sent to battle the Lowes, and as soon as he caught my scent, he would whip around and gallop back for me. I had no plans to hunt the whole day. *Finish this fast*, I told myself, *and go shopping for new lenses for my camera.*

We were in the middle of the city, but the humans wouldn't see us in combat. Another perk of being a Lowe. As soon as we engaged in battle, I became cloaked by invisibility so the mortals didn't know what was going on. And if they happened to see me vanish in front of them, they forgot what they just saw. A little something to ensure people didn't start thinking they were going insane by seeing a girl disappear before their eyes.

And a supernatural brawl could take place in the midst of a crowd of people, and no one would be aware. Both a blessing and a curse.

No one could come to my aid if needed, but no one would see me be a hero either. Still, I kept my distance from a lot of people for a reason—wouldn't want to suddenly disappear in case a monster attacked me out of the blue. People would freak out.

Well, if Heracles crossed my path, he'd see me battle, but he kept out of other gods' business, insisting it was my destiny to eradicate the monsters, not his. That unless he received a direct order from his father, Zeus, to get involved, he wouldn't anger the Olympian god of the sky and thunder and get himself banned from earth.

Oh, well.

We ran through the streets, the clattering of hooves so

loud on the tarmac, I could almost feel it reverberating down to my soul.

He came to an abrupt stop, grunting in the process, looking like he'd hit the horse brakes, then turned his evil eyes to me, empty pools of black that didn't have the capacity for sympathy and compassion the way every human inherently did. A centaur was more monster than man, which was why I had no problem looking the creature straight in the eyes and vanquishing it before it killed anyone.

Even though the humans couldn't see us once we fought, we still needed space. We couldn't do it in the middle of traffic with cars getting shoved about, or hitting the invisible beast and denting a vehicle, without the people inside even knowing why. But it also made it harder for me to keep track of my enemy with so much commotion. And I didn't want innocents caught in the crossfire.

But we'd reached Garfield Park, and I smirked, sidestepping the creature, who'd come to a complete stop. There was more than enough space and only a few humans to get in my way. The grass was lush green and short, and we were in a great clearing, where I drew an imaginary circle in my mind around us.

I would stay in that circle to keep the beast exactly where I wanted.

Taking on a centaur was no joke. The damn thing was as strong as a football player with four legs. This was dangerous in a lot of ways, but I was just as strong. If not stronger. Quicker than regular humans. Still, outrunning a centaur wasn't going to happen.

So I'd battle smart, as Heracles had taught me.

"You know you're not going to win." He snorted, hot air wafting from his fluttering nostrils. Thick eyebrows crowned dark eyes, his lips lined thin, and the only emotion in his gaze was that of death. Mine.

Of course, the downside of having a human side to this creature was that he had a mouth, and centaurs were cocky and arrogant.

"Let's get this over with so I can get back to my life," I called out.

He laughed, the sound grating on my nerves and that only pissed me off. "I've nowhere else to be. We have all day. Then I'm planning on running a rampage through the city, taking as many lives as possible. Should be fun." He snorted again, his lip curling upward. At a fast glance, one could easily mistake him for a Minotaur with his long face, muscular torso, and horns. Maybe this centaur was more deer than horse. But those Minotaur bastards were in a league of their own.

The centaur lunged for me, hooves digging into the green grass, kicking up clumps of soil. Whoever maintained the lawn here was going to have a field day trying to figure out what had ripped the grass to shreds when we were done.

Because the centaur was bigger than me, I had to attack him Matador-style. I was smaller and had quicker reflexes, so I kept him in my imaginary circle, waiting until he was on me before I jumped out of the way.

"What, no sword?" he asked.

"I don't usually take my sword with me when I go shopping." I wished I had weapons, though, as I'd trained with everything from knives and swords to bo staffs and nunchakus. I could hold my own in any battle.

But I also fought hand-to-hand. Or hand-to-hoof as the case may be.

"You humans are so petty with your materialism," the centaur hissed. He spun around to get to me again. A horse could turn on a dime, but with a long body, it took a hell of a lot of effort.

"Never wanted anything?" I asked. "Surely a new saddle would suit you well. Maybe a muzzle while we're at it."

He grunted. "Only your head on a platter."

"Touché," I retorted, jumping around the centaur when he came at me again, staying at his flank as much as I could.

The idea was to tire him out and eventually get an advantage. To strike out. These guys were all about acting before thinking.

But on the next turn, I didn't get out of the way fast enough, and he reached for my head. Dread slammed into my chest. I ducked and threw myself into a forward roll, the swish of air across the back of my head from his swinging hand missing me by inches. Jumping to my feet, I spun around. If the bastard managed to get a hold of me, I'd be screwed. He could strangle me to death. Those arms weren't bred for beauty; the bulging biceps were deadly.

"You're adorable when you try so hard," the centaur snarled. "Almost a pity to kill you."

"What are you trying to do, flatter me to death?" I teased. But my heart raced, needing to keep my head straight and focused.

On the next turn, I leaped out of the way and aimed a kick at his front leg. I connected above the joint, and the centaur stumbled. His eyes widened, wild, well aware of what was coming next.

A horse's legs were fragile on a good day, and they didn't heal quick or well. This creature's weakness was in the legs.

In a change of our little dance, the centaur turned in the other direction, offering me his rear. I dropped to the ground, my face pressed against the grass. The centaur kicked. Air buffeted across my back. A kick like that would shatter my sternum, liquidize my face.

The smell of the soil was in my nostrils, and the Earth hummed and trembled as if it were alive. This was new. Dirt wasn't supposed to shudder, but I didn't have time to focus on what was going on. I rolled out of the way when the beast tried to trample me, and I scrambled up again.

"You're good. I'll give you that," the centaur declared as if he were doing me a favor. "But Heracles didn't do enough. He never does. Your people all die in the end. And you're the last Lowe."

I saw white when he mentioned my family, my entire body trembling with anger.

His evil smile tugging his lips apart revealed yellowing teeth. I burned from the inside out with rage, but he stormed me, the hooves thundering. He knew he could get me this way. The fight was physical, but he was screwing with my head. Ass.

My rage didn't cripple me as he'd hoped. Instead, it fueled me.

I let out a battle cry and waited for the enormous body to charge. Rather than jump out of the way again, I stayed close to the shoulder and at the last second, grabbed the centaur's thick foreleg. Instead of going limp, which would have thwarted me, he stiffened, and that gave me the grip I needed.

I swung onto his back, landing with my legs wide over the horse's body behind the torso. I locked my arms around his throat in a choke.

The centaur clawed at my arms and gasped for air, stomping around. He couldn't buck me off as long as I pulled the body back. I was going to win this one.

But he kept bouncing about. I clung on. My body slipped as he wrestled me to the side, and I slid off his back. As soon as I dangled from the side, the horse body bucked like a rodeo star, and I lost my grip. Blood fled my face as my pulse thundered in my veins.

I was flung to the side and fell to the ground with a thud,

the breath forced out of my lungs. For a moment, I panicked, gasping for air.

The centaur chortled and stormed toward me. He was going to trample me. I couldn't get out of the way fast enough. The ground shook beneath me as those hooves pounded closer.

Before I met my fate, the centaur squealed in a strange, high-pitched voice that wasn't human at all, despair twisting his expression. Then the creature disappeared right before my eyes.

I caught my breath and scrambled up, spinning around, looking for him. What had grabbed him?

A shadow moved between the trees that surrounded the clearing. I frowned and followed the silhouette into the trees. I tensed, preparing for an ambush. Where the hell had the centaur gone? What new trick was this?

Dark eyes turned on me, shimmering red. The man was tall and lean, but he embodied strength. He was dark, and he had the longest hair I had ever seen on a man, but there was nothing feminine about him. In fact, there was nothing alive about him either. A shiver crawled up my spine in his presence.

"Did you kill the centaur?" I asked.

"Yes," he said with a voice that sounded like a thousand whispers all around me, and in that moment, something surged through me. A thundering fire shot through my veins, shaking me at the core. An anger that demanded I destroy this stranger, all rationality fleeing my mind, just the insatiability to destroy him.

"I am Death," he boomed.

"X? What the fuck?" I asked, suddenly terrified. Was this really Death? Yet the earlier anger intensified, but if he came at me now, I would die immediately. I shook my head, trying to clear the anger burning through me, screaming I could take him out. I had to eliminate him this very moment. I gripped the ground around me, bunching up the grass, needing to clear my head.

He laughed, and the sound danced on my skin, brushing against me like velvet. I rubbed my arms, as if that would make the prickly feeling go away, fighting the urge to fight. What was happening to me? Any other monster, and I'd have his head, but this was fucking Death, and yet my instincts were taking over to fight a terrifying foe without strategy.

"I'm sure you know the answer to who I am." He tilted his head to the side, studying me as if I were a mouse and he the lion about to pounce.

And in a blink, he disappeared as if he had never been. The fury rolled off my body in an instant, and I exhaled loudly as sweat dripped down my spine. I remained alone, feeling as if I would throw up. My stomach turned, and I heaved for a moment, sure I was going to lose my breakfast.

When none of that happened, I pushed up, scanned the park, now barren of both creatures, and walked stiffly to my car. I had been loose and comfortable in the fight, my muscles warmed up and my mind sharp. But now, after seeing X—Death had a pet name, how ironic—I felt like I'd been hit by a bus. My mind was fuzzy, and my muscles ached. And how the hell had he made me feel so out of control?

I reached my car, but instead of heading to the mall, I drove to Heracles's place. Shit was going down and fast. I'd never met X before and had never hoped to, but if this was who I'd felt coming to Earth, I was out of my league when it came to facing him.

Heracles stayed in a two-story white house on the outskirts of town with a garden filled with olive trees. He actually pickled them, he'd once told me. I visit his place often, and every time it felt as if I had been transported to Greece.

"What happened?" Heracles asked when he answered the door. Concern pinched the edges of his eyes.

"X is here," I declared, the words blurting out, even though they sounded wrong. Maybe I'd made a mistake. Except I knew that when it came to the gods, they reveled in declaring who they were, their egos always inflated. So I had to believe I had come face to face with Death.

Heracles's face blanched as he let me into the house. My footfalls echoed across the marble floor as I marched to the red chaise longue in the living room and collapsed on the cushions, my legs giving out. A blue sky with clouds had been painted on the ceiling, giving the room a bigger feel. No television for Heracles, just stone pillars at each corner, an elaborately carved coffee table, more lounges. Extravagant paintings of green fields and different deities lined the walls. He never told me who was who, but my favorite was of a young, beautiful woman in a simple white dress hunting with a bow and arrow. I guessed that she was Artemis. This home was a place for entertaining, except I doubted Heracles invited many people over. Unless he had gods popping over frequently.

"You saw him?" His voice grew stern.

I told him about the events with the centaur, how I hadn't been able to finish off the fight. I had nearly died, but I left that part out to avoid a lecture.

"X sends them, so I guess with him here, they won't bother you anymore," Heracles said. "I know that's no conso- lation." He paced around the living room. "Was X alone?"

I nodded, unsure how I felt about the whole idea of the creatures not bothering me anymore. Was that because X planned to finish me off himself? And if that was the case, why hadn't he gotten it over with when he'd had the chance?

"I wonder why Hades wasn't with him. Usually, they're together." He scratched his chin.

"Yeah, I heard that," I said. "I don't know what's going on, but it's big. It's everywhere. I can feel it just like this overwhelming rage to destroy him, my body shaking with urgency. Is that part of the Zeus blessing? Though I'd never felt it with any other creature I fought."

Heracles pressed his hand against his forehead. He looked like he was stumped, and it wasn't a good look on the man I had turned to for answers.

"You have to help me with this," I insisted. "I can't do this alone."

He put his enormous hands on my shoulders, cupping them. Strength lay behind them, and he'd crush my bones in moments if he so chose.

"You must do this alone," he said. "You have to. I can't fight with you, you know that."

"Why not?" I demanded, shocked that Heracles would turn me down after everything we'd been through together, after all the lessons, after he knew my fears and strengths. Sure, he didn't get involved in usual fights, I got that, but this was Death, for fuck's sake.

Heracles let go of me and shook his head. "Because if I join you, I'm declaring war against my family. That will have far worse repercussions rippling through Olympus than you could ever imagine. Unless Zeus directly instructs me to fight alongside you, I can't go against his wishes. These are your demons to face. I will be there to guide you as best I can. I can't fight with you without creating a war amid the gods. I am on Earth as a promise to my father to train you, not get involved. Or he'd punish not only me, but most likely you as well."

I shook my head. "These are not my demons."

"Yes, they are. Your past terrifies you, but you can defeat

them, and you can fight Hades. Zeus wouldn't have chosen your family if he thought you would fail." Sorrow wove behind his words, and I hated putting him in this situation. Heracles was a hero, not someone who backed away from someone in need.

But what if Zeus had been wrong about my family lineage? He had to be so disappointed because every other Lowe in the world had failed. Who said I wasn't next in line to die a tragic death, to ruin a legacy? Who said I could do this at all?

"Maybe I can defeat Hades," I said, highly doubtful. "But if I run into X and we fight, I'm going to lose. He's more powerful than me. There's no question about that." I curled my hands into fists to stop myself from trembling.

Heracles didn't answer me or tell me I would be fine, that I could beat him if I fought smart and hard and dug deep to find my true power.

He didn't say anything because I was right.

CHAPTER 5

Apollo

I didn't know what the fuck Hades was doing in town, but it pissed me off. The whole reason I had come to Earth was because the other gods thought it a waste of their time. They thought mortals were too sensitive and died so easily. Hence, the deities stayed away from Earth, and I lived here. Kept my distance, lead my own life, traveled the globe, and avoided the never-ending bullshit drama surrounding Mount Olympus. Between the three brothers and their three sisters, they were always bickering. The other gods forced to choose sides, which meant a big tug-of-war. No thank you, not my problem.

But with Hades here, he was going to blow my cover.

It also meant Earth would get crowded real soon. Whenever Hades did something stupid, which was most of the time, Zeus was on his heels because he loved being a dick of an older brother. And Poseidon would inevitably follow suit because he was pathetic and had to break up the fight between the two as if they were kids who couldn't be left unsupervised. Honestly, Poseidon had to get a fucking life if you asked me.

No one ever asked for my opinion. That was why I was here, so they would leave me the hell alone.

But I liked Earth. I liked the people. I liked being among mortals. They had so much to live for because they knew they were dying. When you didn't have an end date, when your life stretched into eternity, there was no reason to aim for anything. The idea of immortality was a grand one, but the reality was a whole lot of nothing expanding out in front of me, and I felt lost.

The humans also knew how to love. The gods fucked around. All the time. But love? That didn't happen often. The mortals dedicated their hearts to each other, and romance was cherished. Beautiful.

If I was allowed to love here on Earth, I would have.

Maybe Zeus knew that. Maybe he understood how I had felt love—true love. Maybe that was why the son of a bitch had banned me from falling for a mortal again.

Once upon a time, a very long time ago, when everyone still believed in us and we had been a power beyond measure as a result, I had fallen for a mortal woman. King Priam's wife, Hecuba. I'd had a real relationship with her. I'd been willing to give up everything for her, even my god status.

I'd gotten my heart broken, and she had died eventually. All human women did, which meant that no matter how much I loved, I would still end up alone.

All this time, I'd been living on Earth, allowed to be myself and stay out of the petty god business, but my life had been loveless. It was an enormous price to pay for my freedom, but if all the gods could live with only lust in their lives, so could I.

Lust was on the table. I could fuck as many women as I liked. And I did.

So I wasn't going to let Hades come and screw things up for me. He was an asshole on a good day, but I was a hothead. Everyone who knew me knew that. I could take him if it came down to it. If he played fair.

But Hades had X on his side. Playing fair wasn't always an option. Death went after the souls who had reached their expiration date on Earth. He could do nothing to those whose time hadn't come, and he was shit out of luck against the gods. But X was a dick, and when he and Hades pulled together, it was a childish mess. No one was safe.

I had to talk to Hades before the shit hit the fan. He had to return to the Underworld to his wife. As long as Hades was around Persephone, he kept himself in check.

It wasn't hard to find Hades. The Earth shivered when he neared, recognizing its ruler, and all I had to do was follow the darkness and the fear that emanated from the Keeper of Souls. It flowed from him like waves or more like a homing beacon. So I climbed on my bike, the engine rip-roaring, and took off, following the signal. The motorcycle purred beneath me as I raced along the city road, my thoughts lingering on Hades and me convincing him to leave.

When I found him on the sidewalk, it wasn't Hades at all. I squinted for a better look, then parked across the road. I frowned, looking at the figure that moved fast between the blocks of buildings in the city. He slid along like a shadow, moving his legs like he strolled, but his movements were smooth, as if he was floating. Darkness oozed from his pores, long hair trailing behind him as if it were blowing in the wind.

X. The bastard was in human form. Or at least, as human as he would ever be. Except there was nothing humane about Death.

Why the hell was he here? Why was he not around Hades?

X stalked toward a group of people. Everyone was out. They froze when he neared them. One of them looked up, the young man going pale. His eyes were locked on X's face, and he couldn't move. I could sense his fear spiking like that of an animal who knew he was going to die, and I knew it was because he was looking into the face of Death.

Slowing down, X put his hands on the young man's shoulders, and his friends ran. They didn't wait to help, to fight, to see if he was okay. All but one. The woman who stayed behind looked as terrified as the young man, and her courage wavered. Dread wriggled across my flesh like tiny ants.

X didn't say a word. Didn't need to. He leaned closer, his face inches from that of his victim, and he started breathing in. The man's soul poured out of his mouth and nostrils like fog, and X breathed it all in, consuming, devouring.

I froze, unable to believe what I was seeing. This was all wrong. X wasn't supposed to devour souls. He was meant to send them to Hades, to the Underworld. Why did I get the feeling this man's time had not yet come?

His friend screamed. The shriek was piercing. I tensed, climbing off the bike.

When the young man fell to the ground, his body shriveled, his skin sunken against the skeleton as if he had been sucked dry. I gritted my teeth at the ease with which X took a life.

"What did you do?" the woman bellowed, tears streaming down her cheeks, kneeling next to her friend.

X turned to her and smiled, and the woman and I both knew she wasn't going to last long.

"Run!" I yelled, but she didn't glance my way or acknowledge hearing me, so I rushed across the road, racing across the next block to reach them.

X consumed the woman within seconds, and she collapsed next to her friend.

I hummed with his power. It blasted from him in a wave that rippled across me, stealing my breath. X was stronger than I could have ever imagined.

"What the fuck do you think you're doing?" I strutted toward him, arms stiff by my side. He was fucking with the system.

"Oh, Apollo," X said in a voice that was filled with condescension and pity, as if I were a child who didn't understand the ways of the world yet. I charged toward him, ready to put up a fight. He couldn't kill humans this way. It was against the nature of the gods to take life from the humans when they were still entitled to it.

A sudden breeze blew the dead man and woman away like dust, and there was nothing left but a pile of clothes from where they had been lying minutes earlier.

X didn't turn around and face me. He didn't attack me. Instead, he disappeared in a puff of air.

I unleashed a roar, my voice thundering toward the heavens. I hoped Zeus was watching and had seen all this. His brother had literally unleashed hell on Earth.

When I marched back to my Ducati, a woman stood next to it. I wasn't in the mood for female company. Yet they were always drawn to me, and I adored the attention, but right now I didn't need it.

Her arm was outstretched, her fingers inches away from touching the leather seat.

"Don't," I shouted.

She pulled her hand back and glared at me. The moment she did, something passed between us. An invisible cord. Her eyes were deep, dark pools of mocha that sucked me in. Her hair was long, hanging down her back in a thick braid. Except everything about her screamed *warrior*. Standing strong, legs apart, arms stiff by her side, and eyes narrowing. The energy gleaming off her tingled across my nape. She wasn't a mere mortal.

"Who are you?" I demanded, wondering if she was in any way related to X.

"Elyse," she replied with a defiant tone. "Do you want to tell me what you were doing, Apollo?"

I paused at first, then frowned. "How do you know who I am?" No humans knew who I was. My ability allowed me to walk around on Earth as a mere human without anyone asking questions. But Elyse stared at me as if I were a god, not a man she flirted with.

"Did you kill them?" she hissed, her hand curling into balls.

"Why aren't you answering my questions?" I stood tall, intrigued by this beauty and her feistiness.

High cheekbones, delicate features, long lashes. Full lips. What they would taste like? I wanted to kiss her. Except I didn't often react this way to women at first sight. Sure, I admired them, but this…this was something else.

"I don't owe you answers," she declared, her chin lifted high.

Her defiance drew me closer. So fucking attractive. There was something sexy about her, something that awoke a primal side in me. I craved a touch and not in a way that would be appropriate for two people who had just met. And again, I couldn't understand the sudden lure toward her, but I wasn't backing away. Curiosity had me grinning. Her body was tight and muscular, but she was the definition of feminine. She wore black pants that were so tight, they looked painted on. Her jacket was form fitting, and she wore knee-high boots that were fit for fighting.

"Did you kill them?" She raised her voice, glaring my way.

I shook my head. "No."

"I felt it," she said. "Their death. The magic. I felt it." Her voice wavered, the sorrow lining her words. She cared for the people gods used as pawns.

Who the hell was this woman?

"It wasn't me," I repeated.

Elyse shook her head and looked past me to where the two people had died.

"X," she breathed, her shoulder shaking. "Shit. I have to go." She turned around and stormed away.

"Wait," I called out.

She glanced over her shoulder, and the half-smirk, half-glare was so fucking sexy, I wanted to jump her.

"For you?" she asked in a way that suggested it wasn't going to happen. She carried on storming away. I watched her go. Her hips swung from side to side as she walked away, her body as irresistible as she was deadly.

I shook my head and turned to my bike.

"Nope," I told myself. I wasn't going to go after her. I wasn't going to get involved. Because I would fall for her. I wouldn't be able to help myself, and if I fell for her, Zeus was going to have my balls served on a plate.

When I swung a leg over my bike, the vision hit me. I hadn't had a vision in centuries.

A family, strong and fierce with the power of Zeus burning through their veins. I saw death and destruction, abandonment and betrayal.

And there was Elyse, the last Lowe who still embraced her power, who knew the gods and what they were, who fought for the humans. I had heard of this family, but in the years I had been on Earth, I had never run into them.

Another vision struck me harder than the first.

I was with Elyse, my hand around her waist, her head on my shoulder. We were talking, laughing, kissing, fucking. She was mine, and I was hers. Then she was on my bike, her arms wrapped around me as we sped through the city until the buildings were a blur, and all that mattered was the feel of her skin on mine, her breath in my ear.

The vision finally let go of me, and I staggered, nearly falling off my bike. I forgot how it felt when I was transported to the future to watch what could not be undone. And if Elyse was in my future like that, I was in trouble.

I couldn't let it happen. I had to stay far, far away from her.

CHAPTER 6

Elyse

I couldn't get Apollo out of my mind. Whenever I closed my eyes, I focused on his face, his arms, his hair, his eyes. It was like he was imprinted on the back of my eyelids. And I recognized him at once from paintings at Heracles's place. I had been in the area taking photos for a project when Death's immense power had prickled along my flesh.

There was no shaking that feeling I'd had with Apollo either. Whenever I thought of him, warmth flushed through my body, and I felt it between my legs. What was wrong with me? The sexual tension between us had been so thick, I hadn't been able to think clearly. Instead of giving him any answers, I'd asked him questions of my own. Trying to find out what had happened to those poor humans who'd lost their souls had been the only thing stopping me from being drawn to Apollo and the magnetic allure I'd sensed between us. Of course, this shouldn't have been happening. It couldn't be because no one had ever affected me this hard before.

Yet he had eyes the color of the sky, riveting and seductive. I hadn't wanted to look away, as if he'd bewitched me. His muscular chest and arms had competed with his irises. Apollo had arms that were so big, I wouldn't have been able to wrap both hands around them. The muscles had bulged as if he were flexing for me. His chest had been clad with leather. Long locks of gold had hung down his back, but Apollo was the manliest man I had ever seen. Except there had to be more to him than mere looks because I saw him trying to save that woman. Or was I mistaken?

God help me, I craved him and burned on the inside from being in his presence. Still, even now that I was away from him, I ached for him as if I'd already had a taste of him and I yearned for more. Apollo was like a fallen angel, and I desired him. Hungered for him. Hell, what was wrong with me? I was losing my shit.

Fuck! I had to push that feeling away because I couldn't afford to pine for one of the gods the way I pined for him. Something wasn't right, and perhaps it was the power blessed upon my family lineage. Heracles and the monsters I fought weren't full gods, so maybe the whole attraction-to-a-god thing was a side effect of my power.

I shook my head to snap out of the thoughts that were spinning through my mind. They were all dirty, images of me and Apollo naked, doing things I could only describe as sinful. Yep, it had been too long since I'd been with a man, so I blamed that as well. It wasn't every day one met a god, literally.

Concentrate! X had killed humans, and I needed to talk to Heracles badly. He was my one source, the only person who'd understand what the hell was going on. I had no family to turn to, and I needed to uncover what had happened, how those people had died, and if Apollo had been a part of it at all. Perhaps he'd somehow tricked me into thinking he'd tried to help the humans. Wouldn't be the first time a god had deceived someone. Hermes had tricked my great-grandmother into thinking he was on her side during a battle with a clamor of harpies and that had cost her and my grandfather their lives. It had happened so long ago, I might have been the only person alive who still remembered the story. So, nope, I wasn't going to be fooled no matter how much my body wanted Apollo.

Alarm bells rang through my head because this wasn't me or how I behaved. Or was this the impact gods had on all humans and why they'd thrown themselves at the deities in all the myths? I always wondered why so many women had ended up with gods.

Heracles was at the training center when I arrived for my session. Together, we ran a couple of miles to warm up. While we ran side by side, I talked.

"I don't know what it was," I said when I spoke about the deaths. "I didn't see it happen, but I felt it. It was like they tried to hold on to me before they went or something. I could see their faces, hear their screams. Did Apollo do this?"

"No," Heracles stated out loud. He wasn't even breaking a sweat as we ran. I was fit, but he was half a god. "Apollo loves humans. He always has in more ways than one. He would never hurt them."

So he hadn't tricked me. Damn. I was looking for a reason to hate him instead of fantasize about him. "Then what was he doing there?"

"Maybe he was drawn by the feeling of death the same way you were. You have the power of the gods in you, so you act the way we would."

I was breathing harder as we headed back toward the community center. When we stopped in the parking lot, I leaned my hands on my knees.

"How do I find out what's going on?" I asked.

"There's only one way," Heracles said. "Or rather, three ways."

I frowned, staring at him with my best *go on, talk* expression.

"Come with me," he offered.

We didn't go anywhere. I didn't follow him. Instead, Heracles grabbed my hands, and I was yanked out of this world. The barrier of us traveling into the supernatural world felt as if I had passed through water, and I gasped, squeezing my eyes shut.

When I opened them again, we stood on a plateau of smooth black rock. The sky was shrouded with black clouds that churned ominously. Griffins flew around the tip in spirals. The only lighting came from a river of molten lava that ran from the top of the mountain and past us, the heat almost unbearable, my skin scorching hot, sweat already dripping down my back. Heracles was still holding my hands. He let go of one hand but kept the other in a strong grip.

"Don't let go," he warned.

I nodded. I didn't know what would happen, and I didn't want to find out.

Heracles started strolling toward the mountain with me alongside him. I wasn't sure I wanted to go there. If there were griffins at the top, I was willing to bet other creatures were around too. But Heracles moved forward, and I couldn't stay behind because I was too scared to let go. Glancing over my shoulder, nothing followed, yet my skin crawled.

We approached a pitch-black cave.

"Come," Heracles said as if he knew I was thinking of running away.

"We don't know what's in there." My words squeaked.

Heracles took a deep breath. "I do."

We stepped inside. I trusted Heracles not to lead me off a cliff because I couldn't see anything at all. It felt as if we walked for ages when a flicker up ahead proved there was an end to the cave. As we neared, the cave illuminated by a flicker that didn't seem to come from anywhere at all.

Three old women sat in rocking chairs, wearing black gowns so long, they draped around them, blending into the darkness of the cave surrounding them. They pulled faces as if they were talking or watching something, but there was no sound, nothing to see. Everything seemed wrong with them, giving me the creeps, making me want to look away, but I couldn't put my finger on why exactly.

When we came closer, I realized what was wrong. They all looked up at us, but only one of them had an eye. And one had a tooth when she grinned. More sweat dripped down my spine, and the idea of running away from this place spun in my mind. Why was Heracles bringing me here?

These were the Fates!

Three sisters who took care of the Past, the Present, and the Future of human souls. They foresaw what they controlled as long as they had the eye.

"What are you doing here, Heracles?" one of them croaked. She stood taller than me and staggered closer. Her eye sockets were empty holes in her head. Her skin was like paper, her hair white and cascading down her back, and I wondered what was still holding this old woman together.

"Elyse has a question for you," Heracles said.

I swallowed, trying to speak, but my tongue was swollen in my mouth with fear.

"You want to know about the deaths," one of the other Fates replied from her seat. She was the one with the eye. "X devoured their souls."

"Is he allowed to do that?" I asked, holding myself very still.

"He's out of control. His chains have been broken," the Fate who stood before me explained.

"How?" I asked.

"Love," the Fate said. "It released him and is the only thing that will defeat Death. Am I right, Heracles?"

He nodded, glancing down at his boots.

A fourth woman appeared out of the dark to my right, my muscles flexing as they did any time someone snuck up on me. She glided past us, beautiful, tall and slim with long, curling hair and eyes that stunned me. Who was she? Everything about her was perfect but also deadly.

Heracles squeezed my hand, and I met his gaze. The slight nod he gave me told me not to engage. Yet I turned my attention back to the woman.

She glanced me up and down as if I was worth nothing, and I dropped my attention from her stare. She strode onward, disappearing into the shadows as if she never was there.

The Fate with the eye took out the eyeball, making a squishy noise, and threw it at her sister. My stomach churned when she did. It was disgusting. The other Fate caught it, and it made a sloppy sound when she pushed it into her socket.

"It's not going to stop unless you do something about it," the Fate with the eye said.

"How am I supposed to overpower a god?" I asked, sick of being told what I had to do but not how. Sure, I'd trained most of my life, but my adversaries were monsters and creatures. Not deities. "It can't be me."

"Can't be anyone else. Not even the great hero, Heracles as much as you insist." The Fate sang her words as if she'd practiced them, listened to everything that had happened in my life. "X is devouring the souls, and it makes him more powerful. You don't have a lot of time. No other god can stop him. It's been fated that you will be the only one who can."

"How can that be?" I asked.

"Love is the answer. The thread of life shows you at the center of X's demise. You must find a way to destroy him or more lives will be lost."

So many questions fluttered through my thoughts. I wanted to know how I could stop him and how much time I had left, but we were suddenly in front of the community center again.

I sucked in a sharp breath as if I had been drowning. I coughed, leaning forward, taking more air into my lungs.

"Who was that?" I asked when I caught my breath. "The beautiful woman."

"Persephone," Heracles said. "Princess of the Underworld."

"Is that where we were?"

A simple touch of Heracles's hand, and we'd teleported into the Underworld. Just like that. My gut turned with sickness because people didn't just waltz into that place or leave just as easily. It was where the dead went. I'd read about the Underworld, and Heracles had told me a few things, but it had been so much different than I had imagined. Dark, grim, and depressing. Hell, I sounded insane. This was the Underworld. What had I been expecting? Disney World?

"Those two humans weren't meant to die at Death's hands, were they?" I asked Heracles. "I didn't get a chance to ask."

Heracles shook his head. "No. And the Fates don't talk to anyone, so count yourself lucky to receive their guidance."

"But they spoke to me." I turned to face him, nudging him to look my way. "Why?"

"Because you have to save the world, Elyse." His voice

climbed, the undertone deep and stubborn. He wasn't letting this go.

I shook my head. "I can't. I won't."

Heracles bent his knees and curled his back so that he was my height, then looked me in the eyes. His stare grew intense.

"No one else can," he growled.

After that, silence swallowed everything around us. We kept having the same argument, pushing and pulling with no resolution. So we carried on with our training session, but I struggled to concentrate. My mind was on the Fates, on what they'd said. What had they meant when they'd insisted love was the only way to defeat X? I was the one woman in the world who didn't know how the hell to love. How could I be the chosen one?

When the training session ended, exhaustion swept through me, my muscles wavering. Heracles had put me through the ringer because I hadn't paid attention to his instructions.

"Go home and do your research," Heracles demanded, reprimanding me as if I were a child. "We'll train again tomorrow."

Sick of arguing, I did as he told me, went home, and started reading. Because if Apollo and Hades were already on Earth and X was eating souls, I needed to do something about the situation. The war had started, and even though I was convinced I couldn't do a thing about it, no one else could either.

What would a Lowe do? My father would always say that before a big battle. And I'd respond.

"We would fight."

CHAPTER 7

Elyse

*H*ades had to be stopped. If this was a war, I was going to fight it the way I had been taught. I would do what I'd been bred for. Hades had broken serious rules by letting X loose, and it was my job to make sure no one else on Earth got hurt.

It was a tall order. I was hardly the savior of men, and if I thought about it too much, I had doubts, except I'd trained for this. So I barged forth.

I'd trained with Heracles for years. Long before my father and brothers had perished, I'd been practicing for the day I would have to be a warrior. Fighting was in my blood, and I had the reflexes of a lion. Heracles had made sure I was so comfortable battling, I didn't have to think about it. All I could do now was trust myself when the time came.

After buttoning my leather pants, I pulled on a black long-sleeve shirt while stepping into my combat boots. I pushed my long braid over my shoulder and tugged on the leather sheath strapped across over my chest with two knives and another down my spine. Heracles had made me a nifty bo—a staff used in ancient martial arts practices that looked like a baton, short enough to hang by my side like a police weapon, but when needed, it slid open to seven feet long.

Three knives and a bo might not be enough to take on Hades, god of the Underworld, but I had to rely on my super power as a Lowe, my superhuman strength, and the calling that I could do this to help me through.

Was I terrified? Fuck, yeah, but I was determined to make this work. It was my destiny after all.

Finding Hades was easy. I followed the fear and darkness that oozed from him. His waves pulsed through the city, and I realized how different it felt from X's deadly energy. X was pure death. Hades was only fear prickling on my skin and darkness dimming the day and my thoughts. The distinction wasn't crystal clear, but it was there.

When the wave of magic was so strong, and I struggled to breathe, I found Hades standing in the middle of a barren road outside a school, and he emanated menace. Tall with olive skin and wavy, black hair, Hades was built like a fighter with lean, strong muscles and a perfectly proportioned body. Somehow, I had imagined him with pasty skin like the dead, a body he'd let go. He wore a loose shirt made of a material that traced his pecs and his biceps and pants that hugged his hips like he was doing them a favor wearing them. The god in front of me was drop-dead gorgeous in a very dangerous kind of way.

He scanned the small school surrounded by a metal fence. It was morning, and that meant there were classes. The brick building sat right next to the police academy, but I doubted the cops could do anything about this. My stomach rolled at the idea of what he might have planned to do to the kids. They probably couldn't see him if he concealed himself, and they wouldn't know what was happening until it was too late.

"Don't even think about it," I snarled.

Hades turned his face to me, his dark eyes sharp and bright. Something inside me recognized his power, and the shiver that traveled through me was familiar magic.

"You're a Lowe," he said in a smooth voice.

I nodded. "And you're not welcome here."

He chuckled, and the sound was velvet and warm. I stiffened, not appreciating that I liked the sound of his laugh.

"You're impertinent for a mere mortal."

"You underestimate me," I said. "I'm not a mere mortal."

"Right," Hades said, stretching the word out. "My brother gave you ability, and now you think you're one of us." He laughed again, the sound coming from deep within, his face changing into a vision of unrestrained mirth, and he strolled close to me. "Let me tell you something, little Lowe—"

"Elyse," I corrected.

"I'm not like the other gods. I'm the brother they don't invite to family reunions."

"Is that supposed to scare me?" I asked, even though it kind of did. But that was Hades, right? All fear and nothing else.

Except sexual attraction apparently.

He was still moving toward me, and I held my ground. I wasn't going to run from him. My chest tightened as he moved closer, but I couldn't keep my eyes off him. Hades moved like liquid, effortless and calculated. His shoulders were broad, and the muscles on his neck defined, betraying his brute strength, even though he wasn't built like Atlas.

My hands hung loosely at my side, ready to go for my weapons as soon as Hades reached me. I wasn't going to overplay my hand and look like I would attack while he had a chance to escape.

Hades laughed again, and a trickle of warmth lit up in my chest. I wished he would stop doing that. It was distracting.

"I know what you're thinking," he insisted. "You're going to attack when I'm right in front of you. Well." He moved so fast, I didn't see him. One moment, he was still a few steps away. The next, he was in front of me.

I jumped but held my ground. Hades was so tall, I had to look up, up, up to make eye contact.

"I'll make the first move," he whispered, his voice covering me in goosebumps. He stooped his shoulders and dipped his head.

The atmosphere was suddenly thick with lust. This was meant to be a fight. Even Hades looked surprised about what he felt in the air around us. His face lingered inches from mine, and the churning depths of his dark eyes threatened to suck me in. Our bodies were so close, a sigh would press us together. Fear ran over my skin like a ripple, but that wasn't all.

Sexual desire followed right on its heels, coiling tight in my gut in a wicked anticipation of more to come.

Hades sucked in a sharp breath, and it hitched in his throat. My eyes slid to his lips, and I suddenly wanted to know what this danger tasted like, what it would feel like when my body was plastered up against his. Lately, my body had been betraying me when it came to the gods. First, Apollo. I had thought it was his sultry charm. But now Hades as well? Was it the charm gods had over humans? Except something felt wrong.

Or it was very right, and I was about to make a mistake. It was like an accident I knew was coming but couldn't stop, and I had to keep watching to see how it played out.

He pressed his lips against mine, and my power reached out to his, rubbing up against it like fur, like one monster recognizing another.

The kiss was intense, and I became wet and ready almost right away. Hades pushed the length of his body against mine, and the thick ridge in his pants betrayed that his lust for me was as serious as what I felt for him.

I wanted him. I ached for him. I didn't know what this was or why it was happening, but I couldn't say no. I didn't *want* to say no. We were in the middle of the city, out in the open. It was the only thing that stopped me from tearing the clothes off his body.

Hades must have been thinking the same thing. He took my arm, his large hand wrapping around the wrist, and moved with lightning speed, taking me with him. We were suddenly in front of the police academy, and then we were inside the building. Through the lobby, down a corridor, into an office that was empty and apparently locked. But we were on the other side of the door and alone.

"This is a police academy," I started, glancing around the room for cameras. Except in his company, with us engaged, I'd be invisible too. How else had we just walked through walls without anyone confronting us? I tried to mention how ironic this was, but my voice was breathy, and Hades didn't wait for me to make petty remarks. He kissed me again, hard. My back hit the wall behind me. He covered me with his body, his hard erection pinned against my body, and I moaned into his mouth. I didn't know what the god of the Underworld was meant to taste like, but kissing Hades was an aphrodisiac like nothing I imagined existed. He sank his body lower, pressing into me, trapping me between his legs and hips.

His hand sailed to my throat, so large, I was sure he could take my head off with one hand if he wanted to. But for all that strength that surged through him and the brute force that I knew he was capable of, the hand on my throat was demanding but gentle.

I breathed hard, our lips mashing together.

With the other hand, Hades cupped my breast. He massaged it, and I could taste the arousal between us on my tongue.

"So many weapons," Hades said against my lips. "Sexy as fuck." He fiddled with the leather straps that held the harness around my body and undid it, sliding the harness to the ground. The knives made a scraping sound on the parquet we stood on. I should have been panicked about being without my weapons, should have pushed him away, but I wasn't in danger with Hades. At least, not the fatal kind. I was at risk of giving myself to a god who was meant to be the enemy, but the more he touched me and kissed me, the less he felt like the enemy. Something was happening between us that left me desiring this god like no other.

"Do you want this as much as I do?" he asked, as if finding his conscience.

"Yes." The fierceness of my voice surprised me. What my body wanted and my head insisted on were polar opposites. But more than anything, I had to take the god in front of me. Whatever was going on with us, this was the only thing that made sense. That called to my core. That demanded I pursue him. And my head wasn't foggy. The decision was crystal clear. As wrong as it sounded.

He undid my pants, moving them down as if he had done this a million times. I stepped out of them, leaving my boots on. Clothes were an unnecessary hurdle, and before I knew it, I was naked from the waist down.

I reached for Hades's pants—strangely human for an immortal being—and undid the clasp. When I slipped a hand into his pants and gripped his cock, Hades hissed through his lips.

Good god, he was enormous. And I was dripping wet.

Hades leaned down, and I thought he was going to kiss

me again, but he grabbed me behind the thighs and lifted me. It cost him no effort at all to hold me up and carry me over to the table. He lowered my ass, one arm moving to my back, lowering me in slow motion as if I were delicate. I could get used to this. He nudged open my knees, and Hades kneeled before me, finding my sex with his mouth.

I gasped, my head spinning as if Hades was a drug, dragging me into a sexual need I had never known before. The ache at my core was a fire that threatened to consume me, and I needed Hades to quench it for me.

"You're mesmerizing and so beautiful," he murmured, glancing up at me, his face buried between my legs. And not just any man, but a god.

When he licked me insistently, I moaned. I didn't know who could hear us or who would see us if we weren't invisible, but I didn't care.

Everything had fallen away, but the pure animalistic lust was growing between us by the second, threatening to drag us both under, to drown us.

Hades wrapped my long braid beside me around one hand and tugged gently. I was completely helpless. He had full control, and it should have bothered me more than it did. But the way he stared at me, the passion in his eyes blocked out my world. He claimed me. I surrendered completely.

When he started pushing his tongue into me, I cried out and forgot about everything. I got lost in the arousal, the way he spread my thighs, and one hand reaching over to squeeze a breast. His breathing rasped in and out of his chest, his smooth voice coming in small groans.

I tilted back my head, heat burning through my body, my nipples taut. I needed him. All of him, had to feel him inside me. Each stroke brought me closer and the Earth didn't stop moving. It didn't take long before Hades pushed me toward the edge of an orgasm. Heat filled up my body like I was a cup filling with water about to spill over any second. My body felt like liquid, and I was at the mercy of Hades' tongue.

He licked harder and pumped his fingers faster into me, the rhythmic beat reverberating through me. My moans turned into cries of pleasure. I lost all control, and the orgasm shattered me. Hades pressed his mouth up against my sex, holding, ceasing his movements while my body contracted, shivers racing over my body. I groaned so loud, writhing beneath him.

As I floated on euphoria, my power curled around Hades's, connecting, twisting, merging in a way I didn't understand. But it buzzed through me, sparks of energy dancing between our bodies, back and forth.

"Fuck," Hades breathed. Who would have thought an ancient god spoke like the men all around me?

I had never felt this connected to anyone who'd gone down on me. It had always been physical with the core of who I was removed, watching as if I was a third party. But I had been present and involved here. I had been in the middle of it all. I...belonged.

When my orgasm eased, my body calm. I trembled when he slowly pulled me to my wobbly legs. He was zipping up his pants, his lips glistening. When he licked them, I shuttered, so ready to go again.

"But you didn't finish," I said hoarsely.

"I don't have protection. You don't want a baby Hades running around. Trust me."

I couldn't argue with that, but I was unhappy. The orgasm had been pure ecstasy, it still echoed through my body, and I'd wanted that for him too. So why would he pleasure just me? "Let me bring you pleasure?" I pleaded.

"You have already, but I have to get out of here," Hades said, straightening his ruffled shirt. He scrubbed his face, as if he were coming to his senses.

"Don't—" I said, but before I could finish the sentence, he was gone.

"How am I supposed to get out of here?" I asked the empty office.

My head spun with everything I had felt with the orgasm and the power that had left me drunk. I had to get dressed and get out without being seen somehow.

I was still naked from the waist down, my weapons on the floor next to my bundled pants, and I was in the heart of a police station. Alone.

Well, fuck.

CHAPTER 8

Hades

I swore I would never care for a woman again. Then Elyse Lowe had come along, and I hadn't been able to help myself. Except she had wanted it too. Her arousal had been so thick in the air, the scent had made me dizzy. My need was clear like a good wine, and the effect had shot straight to my dick.

Thank fucking Zeus, the impulse hadn't shot anywhere else. Like this pathetic heart of mine. I wasn't going to fall for a woman ever again.

I had no idea what had happened between us. One moment she had stood in front of me, cheeky as fuck, thinking she could stop me from doing whatever the hell I wanted. The next thing I knew, I had lost all control and caved to my primal instincts. Well not all of them, but I had to taste her until I gained my senses back.

Sex was part of my poison. Persephone had once described me as a beautiful flower or dangerous creature with stunning colors. I drew my prey to me with my sexual allure, and if they touched me, the power ended them. Not by death—that was X's job. But the impact ruined their lives in one way or another. Let's face it, I wasn't a saint.

But the fear and darkness that should have gone with the sexual attraction, the agony and the terror that should have followed once I'd had Elyse, hadn't come. She'd been immune to me.

Yet I hadn't been completely immune to her.

I had wanted so badly to fuck her, to mark her, to claim her. But that would have been a mistake. She wasn't supposed to draw me in, damn it. *I* was the one who lured *her*. And she had pulled on some of my power from the depths of my soul. How was that even possible? It made no sense.

It was a good thing I hadn't. Gods were fertile as fuck, and the chances I would have knocked her up in one go was too great. In ancient times, gods and mortals had children all the time, but this would have been a mistake I wasn't sure Zeus would appreciate, seeing as how the Lowe family had received his blessing.

I arrived at the shitty house I occupied and stormed into the room where I slept. It was nothing like the palace in the Underworld, but at least here I had freedom. The house was an old colonial, abandoned for so long, I doubted anyone still owned the building. Stupid humans abandoned such houses while others of their kind slept on the street. Earth had changed, empty of love, and everyone thought only of themselves. Back in the day, they'd shared shelter from bad weather, split food they'd hunted. Now, people drove past restaurant windows to pick up food in a brown paper bag. Convenience was what they longed for because they worked harder to have more belongings, but at the expense of their loved ones. And this was why I'd fit in nicely here. No love suited me just fine.

From the outside, the structure was awful and I would be left in peace, but with a little magic, the inside had been made anew. Clean of dust, cobwebs, and vermin.

I collapsed on the king-sized bed and groaned. My cock was still hard, and I ached with the desire for a release. Especially with Elyse's sex still in my nostrils. I unzipped my pants. My dick jerked at the recognition of her scent, her power. Remnants of the magic she possessed still clung to me like perfume smothering a fur coat. I couldn't shake it.

I palmed my thick flesh and started pumping my hand up and down. It was a poor imitation of me taking Elyse, but it would have to do. I was wired, and I yearned for release.

With quick strokes, I worked my dick, and I pictured Elyse as I did, that warrior body, her defiance, the way she hadn't been scared of me. The magic that had connected with mine as if we had been lovers once and we were destined to be again.

No! We wouldn't be together. I wouldn't allow it. This had to stop.

Before I let go of my cock, putting an end to the torture that would inevitably come from anything with Elyse, my cock stiffened in my hand, my balls contracted, and thick ropes of cum spewed from the head. I had wanted to empty myself in her body, but it was better this way. Less complicated. My time on Earth was to do as I pleased, not fall in fucking love or get the first mortal woman I slept with pregnant. Let alone a Lowe!

The orgasm continued to rock through me for what felt like forever, my dick pumping out more and more of the stuff as I thought about her and fought with myself about what it should have been, what it should never be.

When it was finally over, I walked to the shower and stripped off my soiled clothes. I opened the water, having seen how technology and stuff works up here on television, and I stepped under the hot spray. We weren't all savages in the Underworld. A sprinkle of magic made everything perfect in an old house. The water cascaded over my body, my chest, my abs, my dick that wouldn't go down as long as she was on my mind.

The image of her face, her striking dark eyes, her mouth that pouted as if she was perpetually pissed off—I so wanted to bite that lower lip—was pinned to the forefront of my mind.

"What the fuck are you doing?" I growled to myself.

I'd been in love with Persephone for centuries. There had been a time when I'd thought we could make it work, even though she hadn't loved me from the start. I had once convinced myself that the admiration that had grown from getting to know each other was as good as true love.

But Persephone's love hadn't been true. It had been forced, an act that could only last for so long. My love hadn't been true either, had it? That stupid spell had caused me to fall for her. That was over now too. All that was left was a fuckload of pain, a promise to never do that again, and a feeling that somehow, I had lost myself.

I looked down at my dick. It had deflated the moment I had thought about Persephone. Well, good. Dealing with a constant hard-on was no fun. It hurt like a bitch in jeans, and it wasn't like I was going to put it somewhere again anytime soon. The time with Elyse had been a fuckup on my part. An unnecessary temptation.

I wouldn't let that happen again.

I washed before closing the water and toweling off. In the bedroom, I picked out a faded pair of jeans and a black tee from the wardrobe I'd filled with clothes. I stepped into boots that I didn't bother lacing up and ruffled my hair. When I looked in the mirror, something about the god that stared back at me seemed different.

"You've been busy," someone said behind me. It was a voice that sounded like it was everywhere at once, a sound that had been my constant companion since my brothers had condemned me to the Underworld.

"Are you still here?" I grunted, turning around to see X lounging on my bed, his dark hair and cloak draped over him like a blanket. His skin had been chocolate before, but it had a grayer quality to it now. He did look like the epitome of Death.

"You're still here." X shrugged. He smiled at me, and his teeth were sharp fangs like an animal's.

"Why do you want to be on Earth?" I asked, striding across the room and checking my phone as if I would have gotten any messages. As if anyone would have anything to say to me. I had a phone because it had looked like a hot commodity here on Earth. But no one talked to me aside from the Fates, who creeped me out. And X, because he was the other half of me, in a sense.

"I taste your bitterness," X declared.

I shook my head. "All you tasted lately was a bunch of mortals who didn't deserve to die. What the fuck were you doing?"

"Is there really a difference between those who deserved death and those who supposedly don't?" Mirth danced beneath his words.

I turned to him. There was a fire in his pupils, the eternal flame that you couldn't come back from. This was new.

"If you fuck with the humans before their time, Zeus is going to be on my ass, and you know how I feel about my brother." I raised my voice, glaring at X, who hadn't moved off the bed.

He laughed, and his chortle echoed through the room. I shivered. Death shouldn't have been able to laugh. I'd never heard him do it before.

"You make it sound like it's something I can control, but this is all on you." He stretched out the last few words, smirking, revealing his fangs.

"Fuck off, X," I spat.

X shrugged again and disappeared in a blink. The asshole had always pissed me off, but there was something about him now that grated my nerves. At least he was gone now. I could get back to...whatever the fuck a god did here on Earth. What the hell did Apollo keep himself busy with when he was down here?

I picked up my phone and pressed a few buttons. It was easy to get the hang of it once I understood the commands. I had watched humans navigate the internet, a database that told them a whole lot of nothing and made them feel empowered anyway. As if knowledge could ever be power.

Only the idiots who had no power used that line.

I opened a browser and navigated to a site called Google. It was inanimate, but the humans treated it as a friend.

Where to tonight? I typed in. I had seen a lot of humans do that when I'd checked on them to see what they were doing with their living hours.

A list of bars and restaurants and nightclubs popped up. Going out drinking sounded like a great idea. I doubted the wine here would be pure like it had been on Mount Olympus, but seeing that I hadn't had that in eons, it would be good enough.

With Elyse and Persephone on my mind, and X hovering over my shoulder like someone reading what I was writing, I needed to have a reprieve. I was going to get shitfaced.

The humans did it all the time. I didn't understand how humans, who had such little time already could spend so much of their lives in a state of ignorance and lack of control. But I was immortal, not human, and getting wasted seemed like the perfect remedy to an eternity of memories that would haunt me.

When I marched into a nearby bar, the crowds parted for me like water, and I made my way to the front. They didn't serve just wine. Last time I'd been on Earth, all they'd had was wine and mead. Now there was a wide selection of alcohol at my disposal. Maybe the humans were on to something.

Either way, I had the time on my hands to drink myself into a stupor. It would take a shit ton more alcohol than it took them to get the job done. So best start drinking early.

CHAPTER 9

Elyse

*H*ades was full of shit. He'd used his power to lure me in. That had to be it. It was the only way I could rationalize the instant attraction I'd felt when I had come close to him. He was my enemy, for crying out loud. I wasn't supposed to orgasm with the gods. I had to fight them. Heracles had trained me to fight, not to dream of fucking them.

I stopped myself from taking that thought further.

It had taken me a while to figure out how to get out of the police academy. The office had been locked, but the windows thankfully hadn't been barred. It wasn't a police station but a training academy. And there were no cameras I could see, and I doubted the training place would have them.

Usually, people said that the gods smile down on them when something goes right. This time, it was a god that had gotten me into that mess.

I couldn't believe I'd let him go down on me or what I had felt when I'd been with him. Hades was meant to be the foe here. Or at least, the person who had released my adversary. X was the killer, not Hades. I knew that, but Hades had control over him, right?

Maybe, if Hades had been purely evil, I wouldn't have been drawn to him, but I had this weakness. I saw the good in people even when it was buried under a lot of ugly. Hades, believe it or not, had good in him.

Still, I was stupid to fall for his antics. I paced back and forth, fire driving my pulse.

I should have been stronger. Should have been able to resist him, but I had trained my whole life to be a fighter. A hard fight against a god with immense supernatural strength was what I'd expected. I hadn't expected the lust, the arousal, the intense need to be with him. And I'd willingly agreed because I'd craved it... Fuck, I still did. And what the hell was that with the electricity between us?

I definitely hadn't expected my energy to rub up against his like a cat. What in the world had that been all about? I had to talk to Heracles. Zeus had given me my ability to fight evil, not to associate with it. I must have missed something.

The more I thought about it all, the faster I paced, curling my hands and digging my nails into my palms to feel anything else but the allure toward Hades.

No, I decided. I wasn't going to talk to Heracles, unsure I could admit what I'd done with Hades. I'd confront the god himself. He was the one who had thought I was someone he could mess with, using all his sexy magic and his body to seduce me when I was sure he would have loved to eat me. Like a snake.

The fact that it had been amazing was only proof that it had all been a trick. Because I doubted I would have loved having oral sex with Hades if he hadn't used his magic to turn me on so much. Though at the back of my mind I kept reminding myself he had asked me and I'd agreed. I'd given myself without resistance. Fuck, it might have been my choice after all, and I wondered if I hadn't just enjoyed our time together because it had been great. It wasn't every day a girl got to make out with a god. *Hell!*

But I pushed the thoughts away because I wasn't willing to accept that.

I set out to track down the asshole himself. It should be easy to find him. Now that my magic had brushed up against his, finding him would be easier. And this time I'd be prepared to not fall for his seduction techniques.

Once in my car, I headed toward where the pulse thumping in my veins told me Hades was when something distracted me. A thundering of magic prickling my skin, different than what I had been focusing on.

The farther I drove, the stronger the new power rocked me to my core. I shook myself, swerving across the lane. Heart racing, I heaved the steering wheel back onto my lane. Thank the gods no one was coming in the opposite direction.

What had that been about? I shook my head because I had a goal, a bone to pick with the god of the Underworld. But this new enchantment was warm, drawing me forward the way a crackling fire drew a wanderer on a cold and dark night, and I couldn't just ignore it. The power in me—or whatever it was that was seemingly in charge these days— wanted to know what it was that I was feeling. I had to know.

"Okay, but Hades after," I convinced myself as I turned onto a side road behind a restaurant. The road led me away from the city and wound through the suburbs. The energy grew, warm on my skin, as if I were basking in the sun, even though the sky was overcast. I couldn't remember a time when the sunshine had felt like this on my skin, or when the sky had been crystal blue without a cloud.

When the heat became almost unbearable, sweat coating

me, and breathing becoming a chore, I parked my car and got out. The source was here somewhere. Had to be. The road crossed over a storm drain of some sort in a bridge-like fashion that was cemented so it made a space where I imagined a homeless person would make a bed. A black motorbike was parked under the bridge instead.

I walked down the embankment as a car flew across the bridge, and when I rounded the corner, Apollo leaned against the concrete wall that held up the road above him. He was smoking a cigarette, the thin stick clasped between two thick fingers, smoke curling from the cherry that glowed red in the dim lighting under the bridge. Apollo wore Levi jeans faded in all the right places, motorcycle boots, and a leather jacket. His long hair hung over his shoulders, and his chin had light stubble on it. It did nothing to hide his perfect jaw, the high Greek cheekbones, the piercing blue eyes. They were teal and almost glowing in the shadows of the bridge overhead.

"Hello," he said with a smile. Apollo's voice was deep and sultry, and I shivered, the sound tugging at something dark and delicious inside of me.

"What are you doing here?" I asked.

"Smoking," he replied.

I rolled my eyes. "I can see that. I mean in Chicago."

Apollo shrugged and dropped the cigarette on the floor, stubbing it out with his toe. He came toward me, all rolling muscles like a beast prowling. His static whirred around me, and it was like lying in a warm bath. I was submerged in the heat that came off him.

"What's going on?" I asked, even though it had been rhetorical. My power was all over the place lately, drawn to the gods in a way I had never felt before. The air was almost suffocating.

"Why don't you tell me?" Apollo asked, cocking his head

to the side. He had stopped circling me like he was checking me out. He was closer now than he should have been. My body was responding to him, even though my mind screamed at me to get out of there. Burning up from the inside, I was losing control again.

I shook my head. My mind grew fuzzy. Was Apollo doing this? He was the god of poetry and music, god of the sun. That explained the fire I felt on my flesh. My energy wanted to roll like a cat in catnip in the heat that streamed from Apollo. My strength almost purred under my skin.

"You should get away from me," I warned. My restraint was starting to slip. Or maybe it already had. I wasn't sure. I only knew if we stayed together, something similar to what had happened with Hades would happen here. How the hell was I going to deal with gods if I lost control around them? Let alone deal with Death if my head fogged up with arousal.

I wasn't sure I was ready for this.

Apollo inhaled deeply, as if smelling my scent, and his eyes changed, turning primal.

"This is my bridge," he said. "I was here first."

I swallowed hard. "Are you in the city with Hades? Are you working together?" I demanded, focusing on each breath to calm myself, to stop the insanity in my mind as I pictured myself with Apollo. A distraction was a must. As a Lowe, I dealt with godly creatures. Sure, Apollo was a god, but what the hell was going on with me?

Apollo chuckled, the sound sweeping over my skin like feathers. "I work alone, sweetheart."

"That has to get lonely," I replied, knowing too well that feeling after losing my father.

"I make do." His predatory eyes never left me. "I can find more than enough companionship when I need it."

I shook my head. "Sex with as many mortals as you like isn't companionship."

I had heard all about Apollo and his love for mortal women. He was on par with Ares, as far as I knew. The gods slept around with each other or with any mortal who was willing to spread her or his legs. It wasn't that they were loose. It was normal for them.

Apparently, it was becoming normal for me too. I cringed on the inside.

Something crossed Apollo's face too fast for me to read. It looked like a negative thought, but he slipped a mask in place that was all charm, and in a few strides, closed the distance between us.

"Let me show you how much it can look like companionship," he said, and his voice was so deep, it came out as a growl.

Fear spiked around me, but heat grew in my core and took over. I backed away from him, but Apollo took another step forward. No denying, I wanted him, and I was sure he could tell, but I couldn't do this. Not again. I had just been with Hades not two days ago. Since then I'd been training, getting my head around what was going on between me and the gods. Although it wasn't the sexual arousal that bothered me. I had always understood the way the gods did the whole pleasure thing better than humans. What bothered me was how easily my power slipped in with theirs when I had to fight those endangering humanity.

Suddenly, my back was against the bridge wall. Apollo was in front of me, his strong, muscular body blocking the way out. The fire that came from his was scorching and wonderful at the same time. Apollo stepped closer and closer still. I lifted my hands and pressed them against his chest to stop him in his tracks.

The corners of his mouth twitched up in a smile. He wrapped his hands around my wrists, and I was trapped.

"Tender is the blossom on the vine. Crushed into sweet

ambrosia wine. A single drop will steal the sweetest breath from your chest." He halted suddenly, his eyes narrowing, his lips tight, as if he'd said something he hadn't meant to.

I raised a brow. "Did you just recite a poem to me?"

In a swift movement, Apollo grumbled something under his breath and spun me around so I faced the wall. He pushed against me and ground the hardness in his jeans against my ass. I groaned when he did, my arousal only growing.

"Sweetheart, I'd give you the world if you were mine. And you can't tell me this isn't what you want right now," he whispered in my ear, kissing the area under my lobe, his tongue licking me. "I can taste your need for me."

I swallowed hard, needing this like I needed air to live. "Don't let it go to your head."

Apollo chuckled, and it was a deep, hearty sound like he was genuinely amused. "You're so hot."

"This, coming from the guy who was throwing off heat like a furnace. Your fiery energy drew me here."

"I'm going to take you now," Apollo said, his breath on the back of my neck.

I should have been afraid. I should have said *no*. I should have fought him and gotten away. But his words melted me, and I yearned for this. God help me, I wanted him to take me.

"Yes." That single word streamed out as it had for Hades and now being in Apollo's presence, he'd transformed me into a sex-starved woman.

He pinned me to the wall with one hand and reached around to the front of my jeans with his other. With quick work, he got my pants down to my knees. The sound of his fly followed, and then he settled the thick length of his dick against my ass, nestling it between my ass cheeks. His flesh was so hot, I moaned from the contact alone.

"I shouldn't want you this much," Apollo murmured. "Somehow you're in my head, fogging all my thoughts."

I frowned through the waves of desire that undulated my hips. What did he mean? I didn't have a lot of time to think about it. Apollo held me to the wall with his hand on my back. With the other hand, he yanked my hips back so I leaned forward a little, my stance widened. He plunged his hand between my legs.

"So wet," he growled. He ran his fingers along my slit, and I cried out, an orgasm already on the verge of happening. Sex was this man's forte. I could tell. And as much as my mind screamed to back away, I couldn't. Like with Hades, I willingly gave myself to Apollo.

When he let me go, I whimpered in protest. I longed for Apollo to push me toward release.

He thrust his dick into me without ceremony, and I cried out as he entered. He was hard and smooth, and he filled me up. I gasped, trembling as Apollo planted his hands on either side of my head against the wall. I stayed in the position he had put in me in. What a good girl I was.

Or a bad girl, because this was the second god in such a short time I was letting have his way with me. And fuck, but I loved every second of their ravaging.

I desired this. I didn't know what drove me to lose all inhibitions, but I yearned for his touch, longed for him inside me the same way I had with Hades.

Apollo bucked his hips, sliding in and out of me. I dropped my head, bracing myself against the wall. I noticed Apollo's legs, how far he had bent his legs to get into me considering his size. But he fucked me as if we were both lying down and it was easy for him to reach me.

Apollo's pounding picked up the pace, and a scream tore from my mouth laced with his name as an orgasm roared through me. Convulsing with pleasure, I labored for breath, riding the pulsing sensation ripping through me. My knees weakened, but Apollo's dick, his hips ramming against my ass, somehow held me up.

The orgasm drew out, one rush of ecstasy after the next. I moaned out, my body floating on the clouds.

"Come for me again, sweetheart," Apollo whispered, his lips close to my ear, and another round of pleasure rolled through me. Electricity hummed over my arms, down my back, skipping onto Apollo.

When I finally stopped orgasming, I was exhausted, and my body felt tender, as if he had ridden me raw. Well, I guessed he had, and I had the feeling Apollo could keep going. He could make this happen for a long, long time.

But he pulled out of me.

"I'm getting tired of you gods not finishing off," I said before catching myself against the wall.

Apollo laughed, and I heard him zip up. "You sound like you're talking from experience."

"Sadly, yes," I said, trying to pull up my pants with a little finesse, even though I felt like I was burning up with a fever from the inside out. When I fastened my pants and turned around, Apollo had strolled to his bike, and he lit up another cigarette.

"I thought gods didn't smoke," I said.

Apollo took a long drag on his cigarette and blew out a cloud of smoke. "Guess you thought wrong."

There was something about Apollo that didn't compute. He sat on his bike, an expression like he didn't care about the world around him, a me-myself-and-I attitude, but there was something beneath the façade that looked different. I couldn't put my finger on it. Something about him, the way his magic had dimmed to a cool glow, made me want to go over there and cuddle up to him. But I had done more than enough that I didn't understand. If I wanted to leave with any dignity intact, I had to do it now.

"I'll see you around," Apollo said.

"God, please, no," I said.

Apollo laughed, another sound that was so calming, it threatened to draw me in. But I fought it and left.

CHAPTER 10

Apollo

I had to stay the hell away from her. Elyse was trouble. After that vision of us ending up together, I had vowed I would stay clear. But she'd come to me under the bridge where I'd been minding my own business. She was drawn to me, she'd admitted. I'd only recently arrived in Chicago after traveling through the country, so clearly destiny drew me here for a purpose. I couldn't even remember who I chose Chicago, but got on my bike and just drove, ending up in this city.

Like my shitty vision had suggested, I had been lured to her soul, which had recognized mine. My power had shuddered, and being with her had felt...right. Oh, so fucking right.

But at the same time all wrong. I couldn't lose my place on Earth because of a woman. She was like every other mortal—nothing special. Which was why I had fucked her from behind, sticking to my rule of no connection and no kissing. That usually worked.

Except this time it hadn't done the damn trick. I had assumed fucking her would get this stupid attraction out of my system so I could move on. All it had done was remind me how much I needed to be with her, with her in my bed and life.

I could date someone like Elyse, build a serious relationship, have purpose in life. Maybe help her with training, as I could teach her new tricks Heracles didn't know. Everyone knew the demigod who trained the Lowe family.

But that was the worst possible idea because dating her would send me right back to Mount Olympus, where I would have to play god again. Lose my freedom to do as I pleased, and when I wanted.

Although around Elyse, I felt like I could wax poetic. I'd write her a sonnet that would do her proud. Not that shit poor one that had poured out of my mouth like something crafted by a lovesick fool. Or I could compose a piece of music that would express what the symphony of my soul felt when I looked at her.

Fuck.

What the hell was wrong with me? Two hundred and fifty years. That was how long I had managed to stick around the humans and not fall for any damn mortal. But Elyse wasn't just any mortal. She wasn't even technically a mortal if you considered the special powers Zeus had bestowed on her family.

But Zeus wasn't going to see that little technicality as a loophole for my pending punishment when I bent the rules. Elyse, no matter how intoxicating, was not worth giving up my life on Earth.

What if X got to her? I had seen the destruction he'd wrought, destruction that he shouldn't have been capable of, which meant something had gone horribly wrong. Seeing that X was practically Hades's tail, it had to be his fault.

The son of a bitch was here when he was not wanted, after all. And it reminded me of Elyse's question about whether I was here with Hades. I loathed the idea of him going anywhere near her because everywhere he went, X was bound to be near.

Elyse was here to protect the humans, and she would try to stand up against X. But X should never have been a threat. The Lowe family wasn't destined to fight Death himself, only the creatures and the gods who were here to mess with the humans. X was out of line, and Elyse would perish if she tried to do what she had been born to do.

I closed my eyes and tried to find a vision of Elyse and X. Seeing into the future was a gift I hadn't used in a long time, but I was suddenly shaking with terror at the idea of the danger Elyse was in—another sign I was going down a path I couldn't back out of if I wasn't careful. I kept searching for future images in my mind.

No matter how hard I tried, I couldn't see anything between Elyse and X. In my visions, Hades was near her, but the son of a bitch always got involved in drama that had nothing to do with him. And Poseidon stuck his nose in too, which made sense. Poseidon couldn't sit back and let his little brother learn from his own mistakes.

Ares also turned up, hanging around Elyse, causing more trouble. I hated that asshole with a passion. He was a loose cannon, and he had to stay far away from me if I wanted to keep a solid grip on my mojo. Though my vision showed who would enter Elyse's life, it seemed blank when it came to her battling X. What did that mean? My visions were divine and, therefore, perfect, so something was wrong here.

When I snapped out of my mind's sight, I took a deep breath and let it out slowly. What was I going to do about this? Finally, I climbed onto my bike and headed for the suburbs.

Heracles pranced about in a Greek-looking house in the middle of modern-day Chicago. Had the guy never heard of lying low? But he had lived on Earth since the day he'd been born, so maybe he knew more about blending in than I did.

When I knocked on the door, Heracles opened wearing sweatpants and nothing else. He had a bowl of cereal in his hand, although it was early afternoon—even gods like Fruit Loops—and he chewed slowly. His chest was bronzed and oiled, and he looked pretty damn godly for someone who lived among humans. Made me wonder again if he really understood blending in.

"So, two centuries and you finally decide to socialize, huh?" Heracles said after he swallowed. He leaned against the doorframe and took another bite, crunching as his jaw worked.

I came clean. "It's about Elyse."

Heracles stopped chewing for a second and beckoned me into the house with a gesture of his head.

The house was decorated in a modern style with a Greek flair. Heracles sat down on a chaise longue, elbows on his knees, taking another bite. I sat down in an armchair that felt way too feminine to be in a room with two gods who weighed upward of two-sixty pounds in solid muscle. The chair groaned when I sat down, so I got back up, pacing.

"What's up?" Heracles asked. He was playing it casually, but the moment I'd mentioned Elyse, his eyes had become sharp and stiffened.

"She can't fight X," I insisted. "She'll die, and I don't mean the coming-back kind." I'd only just met her, but something about her fluttered in my chest. Lowes received bonus lives from Zeus's blessing, but when one was killed by Death, they lost those in a heartbeat and died for real. She didn't deserve that when her future held so many more possibilities.

Heracles pulled up his shoulders. "She can hold her own."

"You know she can't, not against Death himself." I threw up my hands, thumping back and forth on the marble flooring.

Heracles nodded, studying his Fruit Loops intently.

"Can't you talk some sense into her? Stop her from pursuing this?" I insisted.

Heracles looked up at me. "We both know that's not going to happen. She won't listen to me. I'm training her to go for the fight, for Zeus's sake. Not to run away."

"You won't even try?" I snapped, my hands curling into balls. "You're supposed to be her protector."

Heracles shook his head. "Mentor, not a protector. My father never put me in charge of babysitting."

"Maybe that's why your *mentees* all die," I snarled.

Heracles pinned me with a cold stare, his sky-blue eyes suddenly the color of ice.

"Don't you fucking dare," he growled in a low voice. "Do you think I haven't lost people I loved over the centuries?"

I sighed. I understood what it felt to lose mortals, and Heracles had been close to every Lowe who had fought on this Earth since his father had decided to impart divine power on the humans.

"Look, I didn't mean it, okay," I said.

Heracles had his *I-don't-give-a-shit* mask back in place. He put his lips to the rim of the bowl and drank the milk. When he lowered the bowl and put it on the coffee table, he wiped his mouth with his bare arm.

"You like her, don't you?" Heracles asked, his stare intensifying, as if he might be reading my mind.

I shook my head, the fluttering intensifying because Heracles had seen right through me. "I don't want the last Lowe to die out. That's all."

"You've never cared about them before." He took a deep inhale.

I didn't answer him because arguing was pointless. Heracles wasn't an idiot.

"You know," he said, "even though she's a mortal, love for her can be eternal. I had that with my Meg. I still love her so much it hurts. And she's been gone for too long."

"It doesn't matter what love for Elyse would be like," I retorted fast, hating what he implied. "I'm not going there. It will ruin my life."

Heracles shrugged. "If you can fight real love, then you're stronger than I've ever been."

His words lingered in my mind, swirling round and round, reminding me of my vision with Elyse. Together. Joy beaming in my chest. But the longing already haunted me. I couldn't bear to love and lose. It hurt like hell. Not again. I stalked to the door. "If you won't talk to Elyse about X, we don't have much else to chat about. Thank you for hearing me out." Maybe I'd do better convincing Elyse myself.

"Sure. I know you're a lone wolf and all, but sometimes, I could use a drinking buddy, you know."

"For sure." I opened the door and stepped out into a stiff breeze that brought a chill over the city. Some of the gods thought Zeus had been wasting his time with the mortals because they weren't deities, but I sided with Zeus on this and intended to help Elyse as best as I could.

I was purely looking out for Elyse's mortality. Not because I cared for her in any way. I would keep telling myself that. Because if I had indeed fallen for her in no time at all, her magic resonating with mine in a way a soulmate's did, then I was weak.

And that was the opposite of what a god ought to be.

CHAPTER 11

Elyse

*T*he next morning, I woke up in a terrible mood; my head hurt and unease coiled tight in my gut. I was furious at myself for falling for Apollo. No doubt it had been another trick because I had never felt like this around men before.

Then again, none of the guys I'd been with before were gods. I couldn't ignore how connected I had felt on both occasions with Apollo and Hades.

The incidents only confused me. I hated to be confused, and I'd lost control. I kicked a pillow across the bedroom that had fallen out of bed.

I hadn't planned to have sex with Apollo but had merely followed the draw of magic that had felt so warm and inviting. Calling to me had felt so right.

I couldn't explain where the feelings had suddenly come from. It was as if a person inside me, a vixen, had been dormant for so long, and suddenly, this alter ego had awakened. It all started the moment Hades had arrived on Earth. I couldn't exactly blame Hades for what had happened between Apollo and me, but I wanted to blame someone. Anyone.

Despite all the things happening in my personal life—fighting with gods or sleeping with them—I still had a life to live amongst the humans. I still had to earn a living, and I still had responsibilities to fulfill. Right before my world had tipped on its axis, I had signed a contract with *Foundation*, the women's magazine Catina worked for. When Catina had recommended me, they'd bought my photos, and since then, I'd had regular gigs.

I plonked down in front of my laptop and uploaded the photographs I'd taken when I hadn't been distracted by the gods. While the images uploaded, my mind wandered back to Hades and Apollo, how they each had lured me, how my primal instinct went off the charts in their company, but I shook off the thoughts. I had to focus on my human life today. It was hard for me to draw the line between the super-natural world and the natural one, to jump between being a hero with superpowers and a freelance photographer.

Once the shots were uploaded, I started editing the shots of women in urban settings, which would run with articles about the modern woman and where we fit in. I polished the pictures, so they were magazine-ready, but it was a joke. Women were so serious about being independent and strong. "Fierce" was the new buzzword. We were meant to be women who could stand on our own two feet, women who didn't need a man.

When in truth every single one of those independent females wanted men to validate them as such.

It was ironic. But *Foundation* paid me good money for my work, and that was all that mattered. I didn't have to write the articles or offer my opinion. All I needed to do was make sure the photos they needed were the images they received.

My doorbell rang before lunch, and I headed to the front door, half-expecting Heracles to stand before me in Mount Olympus garb, bearing more shitty news. God knew I had received more than enough of that lately.

Instead of Heracles, I found Catina. Her blond hair was pulled back in a ponytail, and she wore a frilly blouse and jeans that flared at the bottom, seventies style. Ballerina flats and hooped earrings finished it off. Why couldn't I look like that? When I wasn't training, I wore jeans and tank tops in case I still needed to fight. And trainers, because no one could run in ballerina flats without getting shin splints.

When I battled, I wore my leathers that hid the black harness and sheaths. You can never go wrong with black on black.

"What are you doing here?" I asked when she hugged me. I tried to swallow my envy.

"I decided to come to you for lunch for a change. The office is so boring today, and you're working on one of our projects, right?"

I nodded as I let her into my apartment.

"Good, so it's like I'm at work." She offered me one of her glorious smiles.

I laughed. "It's not quite the same thing, but lunch sounds great. What do you want?"

In my kitchen, I opened the cabinets, but I'd forgotten to do a grocery run. I had been a little distracted by all the divine testosterone and dick going around.

"I don't have much," I said. "How about ramen? And salad."

Catina laughed and nodded. "It reminds me of college. My roommate lived on ramen. No idea how she ate it every day."

I put the kettle on the burner and waited for the water to boil.

"So, how have you been?" she asked. "We haven't talked a lot lately. I've been snowed under with work."

"I've been busy too," I said.

"With work?"

"Something like that," I replied, lowering my gaze for a moment.

Catina looked intrigued, her eyes narrowing. "Were you mixing business with pleasure?"

What an understatement. When I blushed, Catina opened her mouth in surprise, her eyebrows rising.

"Oh, no," I said. "I know that look."

"You have to tell me everything," Catina said, grinning. "Come on. You never tell me anything about your love life."

I snorted. "That's because I don't have a love life." The last guy I'd dated was sometime last year and it had gone terribly wrong. We had just taken a seat in the cinema when a goddamn manticore had shown up. I'd made up a lame excuse to leave, gotten my butt kicked before I'd defeated the beast, then I'd passed out in a back alley from my injuries. Fast forward to the next day, and my date had refused to answer my phone calls. Who could blame him after I had ditched him? But I couldn't tell him the truth.

Catina shook her head, giving me that look before she interrogated me to death. "Just because you're not dating doesn't mean you're not getting any love, if you know what I mean." She winked, fake-slapping my arm. "Did you know that thirty-two percent of single women have a friend with benefits?"

My cheeks were burning again. Why was I blushing? I never went red when Catina had asked me about whom I slept with before. We talked about men all the time. "That's not true?"

"Yeah, it is. We did a survey with our database of customers."

I rolled my eyes. "What was your sample? Ten people who worked in marketing?"

Catina frowned. "Don't try to distract me. You slept with someone," she said.

Two gods actually. But I wasn't going to tell her that. Catina wouldn't understand it. Hell, I didn't even understand the situation.

"Was it Oliver?" Catina insisted. "I ran into him on the way up."

"It wasn't him," I said with a laugh. Poor Oliver. I hadn't even given him another thought since the gods had arrived. "And maybe he's hanging around because he's stalking me."

"He's your neighbor," Catina added. "And he's interested." She was ignoring my joke. "Why don't you hook up with him? He looks pretty decent."

I sighed loudly. "I don't know, Cat. He's sweet and all, but he doesn't have that thing, you know, that makes my stomach tighten in knots when I think about him."

"And this guy does?" Catina's eyes sparkled. "You have to tell me everything about him. What's his name? I'm guessing he must be super hot for you to go all shy, which also means you like him more than being just a friend with benefits. Who the hell is he?"

I hesitated. She wouldn't believe me if I offered her either of the names. Catina had studied journalism. One of her subjects had included Greek mythology, but even if she hadn't written an exam on the gods, she was smart enough to know who Apollo and Hades were.

"You don't know?" Catina asked when I didn't answer her right away, jumping to her own conclusion. "You're a bad girl." She spoke with a wide grin. "At least tell me what he looked like."

"A badass biker," I said immediately. "With long hair like

spun gold and muscles for days. All leather and cigarettes, and he knows what he's doing."

I took the kettle off the burner when the water boiled, my whole body thrumming with excitement that I'd admitted that out loud about Apollo. After I washed the pre-washed salad out of a bag, I plated the food and we walked into the living room each with a bowl of ramen and the salad.

"Is he a good kisser?"

"I don't know," I said. "We didn't kiss."

"You only fucked?" Catina asked, incredulous.

I blushed when she put it like that, but there wasn't much else to say about it. That was what had happened. Although I had felt more connected to Apollo than to anyone else I'd had a one-night stand with—as if I'd let him into my soul.

"You're going to see him again, aren't you? I can see it in the way your face glowed when you talked about him." Catina stuffed a forkful of salad into her mouth.

I groaned. "I hope not."

"Why not?" Catina's voice climbed. "Sounds dreamy. If he was as good as your blush suggests, you should totally get in there again."

I swirled the noodles around in my bowl. "I don't do repeats. You know that."

Catina rolled her eyes and nibbled on a lettuce leaf.

"I don't get your no-dating policy. What's so bad about being in love?"

I shrugged. It was yet another thing I couldn't explain to Catina. Being in love usually meant eventual marriage. Marriage often meant kids, and kids meant there would be more children who would inherit the Power of Zeus, more people who were in danger of dying, more people I would feel I wasn't able to save.

No, thank you. If not loving resulted in avoiding heartbreak, I would continue the single life. Not falling in love was easier than dealing with guilt.

But not easier to avoid. Especially now that Apollo and Hades were in the picture. How was I going to keep from falling deeper for either of them? They were on my mind constantly, and I jumped at the chance to tell Catina about Apollo. I smiled nonstop when I spoke of him.

But my reaction only made me angry again. Catina had been a distraction away from my brooding mind, but now that I thought about how emotionally vulnerable I had become around both of them, I shook with anger all over again.

"Are you okay?" Catina's brows furrowed as she studied me.

I nodded. "Yeah, I was just thinking."

"About what?"

"It doesn't matter." I took a mouthful of noodles, then glanced at my phone to check the time. "I have to get back to editing. When are you needed at the office?" I hated to push her out, but she asked too many questions I wasn't ready to answer to her or myself.

"Now," Catina said, staring at her watch. "I can't disappear forever. Tina loses her mind, and you know what that's like."

I nodded. Catina reported to Tina, a woman who had PMS three weeks out of the month. I had worked with her directly too. It wasn't a party.

"Thanks for lunch." Catina finished her meal, wiped her mouth, and rushed to the door.

I hugged her goodbye.

"Don't be so uptight all the time," she said. "Let loose, and sleep with your hottie another time."

I forced a smile. *If only she knew.* "I'll call you later."

I waited until Catina reached her car before I closed the door. I marched to my bedroom and took my fighting clothes out of the closet. Dressed in my leather pants and black shirt, I strapped on one harness and took care that the buckles were fastened correctly. I braided my hair down my back and put on combat boots.

Today should have been a day where I didn't think about the gods and all the sexual acts I had been having with them. I had wanted to focus on my work, on being human for a change, instead of focusing on the gods all the time.

But my pulse raced with anger, my heart thumping in my ears, and I still hadn't had a chance to have it out with Hades, to demand he stopped X. That Apollo had been added to the pile of things I had to figure out didn't help, but I could start with the first god who had lured me in with his sexual power and deceived me into thinking I wanted it. Sure, I did want it too, but I wasn't a hundred percent convinced it wasn't some god magic influencing me. So I longed for answers, but also to show Hades I protected this city, and he couldn't do as he pleased with Death, who had already wrongfully killed two people. That was my focus, to make Hades realize I was serious about taking him on if he didn't put an end to Death's attacks. To fear me. And to fucking stop using his lure to draw me to him. Part of my frustration and rage came from my inability to control myself around the gods, I knew that.

But if it hadn't been Hades playing tricks on my mortal mind, then I really had desired him. And I had no idea what to make of that.

CHAPTER 12

Hades

The sun was starting to set on this dazed night. The skies were overcast, and the lighting merely shifted to dim. Slowly, the darkness took over, and finally, I felt at home, as if I were in the Underworld. Night was when I was most comfortable. I wore the night like a second skin, and it made me feel like I was on top of shit.

I had a nocturnal routine most of the time like I was a fucking vampire. Though my devouring of Elyse had been in broad daylight, and I had to admit, I hadn't had that much fun in the sun in a long, long time.

Or whatever was left of the sun after Apollo had abandoned his duties in the city. It had been overcast every day over this city for the past few weeks now. I wondered when it had started getting so bad that even I had noticed.

Not that I gave a crap. I was happy with the miserable weather. I wasn't the god of the Underworld because I loved sunshine and rainbows.

"Hades!" someone shouted from outside my house. My body responded to her voice, standing without thinking.

I opened the door and pushed my hands into my pockets, grinning at her as she stood on the sidewalk. What, she didn't even have the guts to knock on my door?

"Did you come for round two?" I teased. Immediately, I regretted making it sound like it was all about getting some ass. But, Almighty Zeus, her ass was delectable. Eating her out had been the best thing I had done in centuries.

"I'm not here to banter with you." With her head held high, she kept her composure, her arms tight by her side, her hands curled. But I saw the way her eyes had widened when I'd opened the door, the quick gulp of air she'd sucked into her lungs.

"You're angry," I said. "I like angry."

"Yeah? Come down to the sidewalk, and let's see how much you like it."

Fuck me, she was sexy. She was clad in leather as she had been before, and she had her knives and sword in their sheaths on her body. There was nothing more orgasmic than a woman who knew how to wield a weapon. I had a thing for warriors.

Which was how I had known from the start that my love for Persephone had been a spell. She had been as delicate as a flower.

And I stomped on flowers.

Now with Elyse in her combat mode, I couldn't help myself. She was pissed off about something, but she drew me like a magnet, and her power was mesmerizing. I wasn't sure what it was, but I had to go to her. I walked down the steps of the house that looked like a derelict piece of shit on the outside. All other homes around us had been abandoned, so it was just us on a street with trash blowing in the wind, tree branches rustling along the front yard.

"What do you want, princess?" I asked.

"I'm not your princess," Elyse hissed through gritted teeth as she grabbed a short baton that hung from her belt.

"That's your weapon of choice?" I barked a laugh. "You're dreaming if you think that's going to do anything."

"I guess I'm a dreamer." She wielded the baton in front of her almost like a sword, and suddenly, it was a seven-foot bo with a steel tip that had been forged into a very, very sharp point.

I jumped back.

Elyse smirked, and it was a smile full of menace.

A woman after my own heart.

She ran toward me, the bo above her head. She planted it on the ground a few feet before me and launched into the air. Using the bo, she vaulted toward me. Strong and fast. I barely managed to get out of her way.

"You seem like a decent fighter," I said. "I like it."

"You won't like it for long." She swung the stick around, lashing out with her back leg and kicking me on the knee. I hadn't expected that. Truth be told, I'd been fascinated by her skills. But she was attacking me, not someone else. If she beat me, I wasn't going to enjoy the show nearly as much as I would have had I just been observing her.

"Motherfucker," I bit out as I sank to the ground for a second until the pain subsided. It was a sharp ache, but I was the god of the Underworld. The pain was inconsequential.

"If you want to fight me, fine," I said, and my two-pronged fork materialized into my hands. It was made of metal with gems along the length of it, and it breathed as I touched it. I was also the god of the Earth, so metals and precious stones were mine to control. On our last meet, we'd kissed, but that had been the magic between us, drawing us closer, and now she wanted to kill me. Why? Because she blamed me for something I didn't do? Wasn't that the story of my life.

Elyse let out a battle cry and lunged for me again, swinging the stick overhead first, attacking with a kick and then following by sweeping her bo low to the ground to knock my feet out from under me.

It would have been a great move if I weren't stronger and faster than she was. Even with her Zeus-like powers.

"You forget that Zeus is my brother," I said. "We grew up fighting."

I ducked when she aimed for my head and blocked two punches with my pitchfork.

"Yeah, I can tell who lost," Elyse said.

She wasn't even breaking a sweat, and she moved hard and fast. I would have been impressed if she hadn't almost nailed me.

"Your power isn't close to being equal to that of my brother. I won't lose to you," I growled.

"Is that why you took me into that office in the police academy?" Elyse asked. "Was that a battle tactic?"

"That was a moment of weakness that won't happen again, trust me," I said. "I don't make the same mistake twice."

"Good. We wouldn't want you to end up with a woman who doesn't really want you, now would we?"

Her words were a lot deadlier than her weapons. Fuck the internet for allowing the world to know everything. Anyone could read about my failure as a man who loved a woman who could never love him in return.

I was such a pussy. Her words shouldn't have gotten to me. But they did, and I trembled with fury. I was immortal, so time didn't matter, but I had wasted years trying to make Persephone see I was worth loving. What hurt more was that for a while, I'd thought it had worked. I had believed I'd managed to get her to love me back.

But it had all been a lie.

I screamed, reaching for the bitterness that swirled in the pit of my stomach, and ran full-speed toward Elyse, my pitchfork lifted over my head, ready to skewer her. Darkness rode on the wind with me, blocking out everything—the scenery around us, the city lights, everything that could mean something. Being shrouded in darkness was when I felt nothing. It was where I was at peace.

My pitchfork hit something, and it wasn't the result I had expected. The weapon obliterated anything in my path. Elyse and her bo shouldn't have been able to block my attack.

We stood opposite each other, our weapons almost merging with the power that trembled through both of us. She was powerful. I had to hand it to her. This wasn't just Heracles's training. This was a power Elyse possessed that was all her own.

Her power lurked right beneath the surface, not fully realized. It peeked at me with eyes that promised torment if she realized how powerful she could be. But she wasn't there yet. I was still a god, and Elyse was only a mortal.

Metals were mine to control, and I yielded that power, twisting her bo out of her hands and knotting it up like the stem of a cherry.

Elyse's eyes widened, her mouth dropping open, but she didn't miss a beat. She snatched two knives from the sheaths across her chest and came at me samurai-style, her weapon over her shoulder, charging. Heracles had covered every fighting style, hadn't he? It was beautiful to see her in action, a dance I could sit back and admire for hours.

The blades cut through the air. She was riled up, and rage drove her. I spun out of the way every time, allowing her to slice a piece of my clothing to let her feel like she was doing something worth her while. She was strong, but I was much stronger.

But I could sense her anger burning off her, her resentment.

This fury that would end up killing her. It was uncontrolled, wild.

"You shouldn't pick a fight," I said.

Elyse breathed hard.

"You shouldn't play dirty," she reprimanded in an icy voice.

"How am I fighting dirty? You have the power of Zeus in you. If anything, this is fair."

Elyse shook her head and threw one of the knives at me. I lifted my hand and stopped it. The knife floated in midair, the point only a fraction of an inch away from my throat.

"Tsk, tsk." I clicked my tongue. "Don't you know you can't kill a god?"

"Not with weapons forged by men, but I can send you away from the Earth with weapons forged by gods." Mirth weaved through her words.

I frowned and snatched the blade out of the air.

"This knife was crafted by Ares!" I boomed. "Where did you get it?"

"I have contacts on Mount Olympus, but I guess you wouldn't know that, would you? Not having been there for so long."

I gritted my teeth. "You're a bitch, you know that?"

"Am I to assume you don't like that? Or is that another backhanded compliment?"

"You're starting to piss me off," I said, and I hurled the fork at her. If it pierced her chest, she would die. Elyse had more than one life, but at least killing her—even if just temporarily—would be satisfying for a while.

Elyse threw herself out of the way despite the strength with which I had tossed the weapon.

"Is that the best you can do?" she mocked.

"No, I can do better," I said. "That includes when it comes to finding sexual partners."

It didn't take her long to figure out I was referring to our little romp, and her sexy mouth twisted. Her power spiked as a result, sending a ripple through the atmosphere that tightened my chest. Bitch or not, this woman was powerful, and it was damn sexy. I couldn't help it. My dick punched up in my pants, her technique turning me on, and the sexual tension thickened the air.

"There you go again," Elyse said. "Do you think sex is going to win the fight for you this time?"

"Do you want to find out?" I was horny as fuck, and I wanted her on her back. I wanted to strip her clothes off and display that toned body, riding it raw until neither of us could fight anymore.

"Son of a bitch." Elyse pulled out a short sword from her back. How many weapons did she conceal? How did a slight little thing like Elyse Lowe walk around town armed like an executioner and get away with it?

But she was part of our world. Elyse was divine in certain ways, and like us, she had shields that stopped the humans who weren't close to her from seeing what she really was.

That didn't stop the gods, and I knew what she was. She was a woman who somehow, despite her sharp tongue and low blows, had me by the balls, and I wanted her. Every fiber in my being screamed for her.

Which meant it hadn't been a one-off thing and I was in deeper shit than I thought.

CHAPTER 13

Elyse

*H*ades didn't have his mind on the fight. No doubt, his thoughts were on what we'd done the last time I had attempted this. It was his downfall—I wasn't distracted by his body or his sexual skill at all. No matter how incredibly attractive he was. There was something so hot about Hades's darkness that made me feel like I was dancing with danger. I guess I had been flirting with death recently.

But today, I was too pissed off for any of that to matter. Hades's appearance on Earth had unleashed Death and people were dying.

Besides, the gods were messing with me, and I didn't know what was going on. The ignorance bothered me more than them poking their heads into my life. I wasn't one to give up good sex with anyone, not even two drop-dead gorgeous gods. But their motives scared me. They had their own reasons, usually at the expense of humans, so was I being drawn into a more sinister god-related problem? Their control over me and the magnetic draw I couldn't ignore had me terrified.

I was a fighter with divine abilities to protect the humans and battle mythical creatures. I wasn't going to let the best attraction I had never felt before come between me and my destiny. Dad would have been proud of me for facing such a powerful adversary.

When I pulled the short sword from the sheath on my spine, Hades's eyes widened a little. He hadn't expected that. Good. Surprising my opponent was one of the things Heracles had always emphasized.

With the sword over my head, I ran toward Hades. I let out a cry born from the rage inside of me. My heart thundered in my ears and adrenaline pumped, pushing me to be faster and stronger than I already was.

I reached Hades and brought the sword down, aiming for the soft spot where the neck and shoulder met. Hades couldn't die, but he would go down hard, and pain wasn't only a mortal flaw.

But at the last moment, he raised his pitchfork. My sword hit his weapon with a terrible squeal and bounced back. The numbing shock traveled up my arms, but I absorbed the strike, reaching deep inside for my power.

I circled the sword and brought the tip down again. This time, the energy within pushed forward with my blow. The blade sang through the air, humming with magic. Hades lifted his pitchfork again, but the blast as the weapons collided threw him backward. Wow, that had stunned me too.

He ended up on his ass on the tarmac. I laughed bitterly.

"Not so hot now, are you, big guy? Even the god of the Underworld can fall on his ass."

Hades rose without a word as if his concentration were solely on the fight, not smartass comments. Okay, he didn't push himself up as much as he was suddenly upright again, and the vibes that rolled off him were darker than ever. It was as if the blackness consumed everything, dancing on my skin, creeping toward my face, making breathing hard.

But there was warmth to the darkness, a recognition that I shouldn't have felt. I wanted to pull the sensation around me like a cloak and roll in it.

When Hades came toward me again, his power preceded him, and it pushed against me like a giant hand. Terror gripped my gut, and I knew he could trample me. Squash me like a bug. He was a god. I was nothing but a human with a bit of zap that Zeus had decided I was allowed to play with. I suddenly realized how poorly matched this fight was. Hades was fucking way out of my league.

He came at me, and something on his arm moved. It was hard to see what in the darkness. His movement was different too. It was fluid, reminding me of something but not water. Something more sinister. Something…snakelike.

The moment I thought of the reptile, I knew I was looking at a viper on Hades's arm. I didn't know what kind, but the creature was wrapped around his forearm. The head rested on his hand as if it were a pet. It was a manifestation of Hades's authority. The snake was his symbol. The serpent wasn't real.

He raised his pitchfork again, and this time, the strength that came with him shifted the world around me. We were removed from reality, somehow. I still had both my feet firmly on the tarmac, the shitty house where Hades stayed to the side, but we weren't quite in touch with Earth anymore.

Then we weren't on Earth at all. We were in the Under-world. After going with Heracles when we'd spoke with the Fates, I recognized the darkened, murky world. But Heracles had held my wrist to bring me here, yet Hades had brought me here through strength of will alone.

But he didn't need an advantage in our battle... this was pure and simple him flexing his muscles, showing me I stood no chance against him. Well, that was where he was dead wrong because I wasn't backing down.

No matter how thick the fear was in my throat. Heat rushed up, burning me from every direction. We were much closer to the river of lava than I had been with Heracles.

Hades glided toward me again. His face remained his, handsome and beautiful. But another face peeked out from the surface. Dark and twisted. The face of a monster.

X?

But it couldn't be. X was on Earth. I knew that for a fact—unless he'd teleported here just as quickly as we had.

Hades threw his pitchfork at me like a spear. The weapon obliterated anyone in Hades's path, according to stories I'd read. My heart thudded in my chest. I jumped to the side, and the thing narrowly missed me, the air rippling across my arm as the pitchfork flew past. But I neared the lava with each stumble. Everything hurt, becoming almost unbearable as I swore the molten river heat was cooking me alive. My feet scorched from the smoldering ground that sent me into a disorientated haze. I lifted my arm to shield my face from the fiery sizzle. Sweat trickled down my neck and back.

"Are you still having fun?" Hades asked, his voice menacing.

I only had the sword with me. The remaining smaller knife and my bo staff lay on the tarmac on Earth—however far that was from here.

But I refused to let him defeat me. Dad used to say that sometimes showing confidence to an opponent was half the battle won. Right now, I trembled from uncertainty while heat from the lava licked at my burning face and curled around my body. Using what I had, I launched forward and thrust the sword toward Hades. He evaded me, but the sword nicked the skin on his arm. Darkness leaked out of the cut instead of blood, as if Hades were made of shadows.

"I'm getting bored," he snarled. He thrust the pitchfork at me again, but I blocked it easily. His fist followed, clipping me on the jaw, and I stumbled. It fucking hurt, vibrating across my head, and stars danced in my vision, but I recovered. Quicker than I should have if a god had punched me with full force. There had been more magic behind the punch than momentum, and magic, I could handle.

Hades was pulling his punches. He was stronger than me. He was a god, for crying out loud. Shit, look at where we were purely because almighty jerk Hades had willed it so.

But I wasn't losing and I wasn't dead yet.

He was letting me think I could win.

Asshole! I heaved each breath, hating how he toyed with me.

"Am I not a worthy opponent?" I shouted as I swung my sword again.

Hades blocked the attack easily with his pitchfork.

"Am I too human for you?" Another blow accompanied my words. Hades was deflecting but not fighting back.

"What the hell is your problem?" His brow pinched with anger.

I didn't attack again. My chest rose and fell, my breathing labored, and the scorching fire was sapping my spirit. I swayed on my feet, my mouth parched.

"What makes you think I have a problem with you?" Hades demanded, his shoulders curling forward. "You're just a *human.*"

"That didn't seem to bother you before," I replied.

Our battle had gone from physical to verbal, and suddenly, we were on Earth again. The reprieve from the heat was instant, and I nearly cried with relief. My body was numb, like the times I'd drunk Slurpees too fast.

"Don't tell me you're hung up on our little encounter," Hades said. "I know it's hard to hear, princess, but you're not my type."

I squared my shoulders because I'd be damned if I let him get to me. They were words and nothing more. "What is your type? Unattainable?" A pinch of guilt twisted my chest at my words, but I kept my head high, refusing to show him. He was the enemy, after all.

Hades's features darkened. In literature, there were a few different accounts of his relationship with Persephone, but no matter which one was true, I knew it was a sore point for him. So I'd hit where it hurt.

"I can't tell why no one likes you," I added. "You're such an approachable person."

"You're a real piece of work," he snarled. His eyes drowned deep, pits of black rage. I should have been scared, but the relief from the heat that had rushed back now that we were on Earth made me giddy.

"Courtesy of Zeus," I said. "You may rule the Earth, but you only get control over humans after they're dead, and by then, it's too late. Pity that you got the entire planet, but you still didn't get the people to rule over."

Hades grew angrier and angrier, his face redder, his eyes narrowing, his posture curling forward. I was baiting him. I wanted him to come at me. Wanted a real battle, one where he didn't treat me like a girl. I didn't intend to win because he'd let me. I'd defeat him because I was strong enough.

Even though I knew it was only my anger speaking, I doubted I would ever win against a god. But I wasn't backing down or showing him weakness.

I launched for Hades again, but he didn't even deflect this time. He merely stepped back.

"Why won't you fight me?" I shouted. "Why don't you treat me as a real opponent?"

"Because you will never be my equal." His voice became calm, his expression almost tiresome.

The rage flared up inside me again, and I could feel it ignite my ability, which now sizzled up my arms and legs. Adrenaline charged through my body. I trembled, strung as tight as a bow, so I rushed toward Hades again, intent on putting an end to this, to prove him wrong.

Except his power flared up as soon as I came close, like an invisible wall, and my magic recognized his, withdrawing.

Instead of clashing, instead of fighting, our energies reached out for one other. They tangled and rubbed against one another like giant cats, just as they had the other the day in the police academy.

With the recognition came the sexual tension. The atmosphere grew so thick with lust, I could barely breathe, and I was out of breath for a different reason. Fiery steam rolled off my body, and Hades met that burning with a flare of his own. It replicated the singeing heat from the Underworld, but this was different…it was welcoming. Caressing me, not threatening to cook me like a shish kebab.

Hades stepped closer to me, and the connection between us grew stronger, threatening to take me over, bubbling over my skin like static. I longed for him to drag me into his house and make me his. When I stared up into Hades's eyes, his gaze swam with hunger for me.

But I fought the temptation, clenching my jaw, picturing Death and what Hades had unleashed on Earth. I couldn't let him take me again. I would only let him win if I did.

Except this wasn't Hades's energy turning me on. This wasn't his sexual lure that drew me in so he could defeat me while I was drunk with the need for him. This was different. I stood before him with my own power, and the sexual charge that only grew between us was real. No illusion here.

Hades stood so close now, our bodies' forces entwined,

prickling over my skin. The invisible energy pushed me toward him, so it seemed only natural that our bodies would follow. My lips were parted, my breathing shallow, and I was getting wet. Hades licked his lips, his tongue darting out, and I yearned for his kiss.

His eyes slid to my mouth, but I couldn't let this happen.

If I had sex with Hades, it would be because of what I felt and not because of what he'd made me feel. Something about him called me, and my power cried out to be with his. It struck me in the chest, squeezing my lungs, squealing in my ears like warping metal.

And this recognition that our magic connected scared the shit out of me.

I forced myself to take a step back. Another step, followed by one more. I swayed, pulling away from him almost crippled me, shaking me to the core. But I recoiled farther still, my legs shaky, my mind screaming to return.

"Don't go," Hades said in a whisper that sounded as if his words rang in my head.

"I can't do this," I pleaded.

Instead, I turned around and ran.

CHAPTER 14

Elyse

I only noticed the sunrise when I was on my way to Heracles. I hadn't realized Hades and I had fought through the night.

The sky started to color, and for a change, there weren't so many clouds in the sky that the sunlight was blocked out. A line of gold shimmied across the horizon where the sun would appear eventually, driving the darkness away.

The symbolism wasn't lost on me. I had managed to get away from Hades, Prince of Darkness.

But I couldn't be emotionally attracted to him. Hades was the god of the Underworld, for fuck's sake. He had released X. I didn't get the idea he had done that on purpose. As much as I wanted to believe Hades was the enemy, I struggled to see him entirely as a bad guy. But yesterday, I'd been fuming because I'd felt tricked into falling for him, and during the battle, he'd treated me like an insignificant fly he could swat whenever he felt like. Arrogant much? Sure, he was a god and all, but his attitude still bugged the crap out of me.

He was full of shit. He cared only about himself. He might be as attractive as hell—har har—and he knew it. He used his magnetism. But there was something about him, something buried under the conceited façade that was...lovable.

Oh, god. The moment I thought it, I felt like I was going to throw up.

What if the time we'd spent together hadn't been about Hades's way of drawing me in but something different? Something real? How was I supposed to handle that?

And what about the sex with Apollo? I was acting like the gods, sleeping around like they did. What did us sleeping together mean to them, and what did the romp mean for me?

The only person I could turn to about this was Heracles. We weren't exactly on those terms. If I wanted to talk about boys and sex, Catina was the friend I turned to. But how was I supposed to explain that to her? Hey, I slept with a god and let another one go down on me, and I'm not sure if they made me want it or if I wanted it all by myself. Yeah, sure. That conversation was going to go down horribly in a myriad of ways.

Not only would Catina not be able to help me, she would think I was certifiably crazy.

There were days lately when I wondered about that myself.

I knocked on Heracles's door. I kept striking until he finally opened because I had obviously woken him up. His long hair was a mess, his eyes swollen, and he scrubbed his face with his hand, then yawned.

"What's wrong?" he asked when he looked at my battle clothes.

I pushed into his house and past him, even though he hadn't invited me in.

"I don't know what's going on," I said.

Heracles closed the door behind me.

"Whatever it is, can it wait for coffee?" he asked. "The sun is barely up."

I nodded, and Heracles dragged himself out of the room. I followed him to the kitchen. It was a large room, two stools against a counter island in the middle with a bowl of fruit atop it—as if he ever had company here. I plonked down on one of the stools and watched Heracles while he moved around the kitchen, putting a new filter in the coffee machine and filling it up with beans.

"I'm pretty sure it was the gods who came up with coffee," Heracles said, yawning, one hand scratching the stubble on his cheek while he pushed the button and the machine percolated to life.

I laughed because if you asked Heracles, the gods invented everything. "I thought only humans couldn't function without coffee."

Heracles shrugged. "The struggle is real. What do they say these days? Hashtag."

I smirked and glanced across at the Danito's Pizza box. Well, seemed Heracles wasn't all into healthy food, but then again, he could probably eat junk food twenty-four-seven and never gain a pound.

"What's up?" he asked, his eyes tender, as if he were ready for whatever news I would lay on him.

"Your coffee isn't done yet."

"Tell me anyway." He tucked his hands into the pockets of his pants.

I took a deep breath. "I made out big time with Hades, and then had sex with Apollo." Biting my lip, I looked at Heracles as he blinked at me. What was he thinking? That I'd had zero control and fell into bed with the first gods who crossed my path?

"I thought you were fighting Hades," Heracles asked without a hint of emotion in his voice. Was he not surprised?

I sighed. "Me too. I don't know what's going on with me. At first, I thought it was him. You know, his allure thing. But I went to pick a fight—that's where I came from—and it's not that."

"You're attracted to him?" Heracles asked in his fatherly voice.

I nodded before I buried my face in my hands, burning up and never wanting to face Heracles again. In my head, I sounded like a weak teenager who was boy crazy.

"Both of them," I mumbled through my fingers. "What does that say about me?"

The nutty aroma of coffee filled the room, the gurgling sound of the coffee machine interrupting the silence between us. I hadn't ever talked to Heracles about sex. I wasn't sure what his thoughts were. He was part god, so he'd seen the craziness that deities got up to, but this was me. Heracles knew my father, my family, my ancestors. "Had any of my family line fallen for a god?"

"Not that I know of."

I sighed. "I'm sleeping with the enemy, aren't I?"

"No," Heracles said matter-of-factly.

"Why not? Are they not my adversaries?" I lifted my gaze.

Heracles shook his head. "It's not that simple. Hades is causing trouble here, but the gods aren't exactly destructive. We're here to look out for the humans, after all. It's X that's really the problem, but he's Death, not a god. The gods had a lot of drama, and Hades being here isn't good news, but it's not exactly about defeating him."

"Then I don't get it," I said. Why did he get me so riled up to the point where I wanted to punch him in the face?

"I don't know how to explain it. See it as a love-hate relationship."

"How do I handle my feelings then? I haven't been with

anyone in a while. I mean sex, sure. But this is different. This is…"

"Emotions?" Heracles asked, cocking a brow.

I stared at him, feeling like a fool. I'd always tried to present myself as strong to Heracles, to show him I was growing as a warrior, learning from him, yet I'd come to him with a love problem. "I'm being an idiot, aren't I?"

Heracles stood up and walked to the machine. The coffee wasn't ready yet, but he switched it off and poured two mugs from the bit that was available. He added milk and sugar to both and brought them back to the counter island where I sat. I took the hot mug from him and blew the steam from the top of the cup. The liquid scalded my tongue, but it tasted amazing. Nutty and sweet. Maybe Heracles was right about coffee being from the gods initially. It was right up there with tiramisu.

"Your power is drawn to the gods," Heracles explained as he sat next to me. "It's born from the same place, after all. I'm not surprised there's something there. Don't fight it."

"So, what? Sleep with them all?"

Heracles sipped from his cup, cocking a brow. "Is that the only alternative?"

"Feels like it with these two," I said with a groan, remembering how incredible they made me feel, how much I craved them.

"We don't see sex the way humans do. It's as normal to us as breathing. Sex and love aren't the same things to us. Far from it. So I don't think all this is so strange. And you'll do better if you let yourself be who you are instead of fighting it."

"So sleep with them all," I said again.

Heracles chuckled, the sound booming through the kitchen as if my ridiculous suggestion had caught him off-guard. "If that's what you want."

I shook my head. "It doesn't make sense. I've never viewed relationships the same way my friends do, but this is a bit extreme, even for me." Yet I couldn't help myself around the two gods.

Heracles shrugged. "As soon as you realize there are no rules, you're a lot freer to be yourself."

I nodded, and we sipped our coffee in silence. I thought I understood what Heracles was trying to tell me, and I appreciated that he was going out of his way to humor me with some girl-talk. To gods, sex was an act of bonding, like a bonding embrace maybe, but it was a million times more intense and personal for me. So was I overthinking this?

Except my situation with Apollo and Hades didn't seem as simple as I had made him think it was. This wasn't only about sex. Whatever it was I had felt with Hades had been real. There had been emotions. I had felt more than the need for our bodies to collide, and I had no idea what to make of that. Heracles wasn't talking about something like love. He was talking about pure lust.

And what about Apollo? Now that I had felt this whatever it was with Hades, I wasn't sure that what had happened with Apollo had been purely physical, either. In fact, it had been so much more with Apollo. When I thought about him, the warmth that defined his power rolled through me, called to me, made me long for him.

Hades was hot because he was dangerous, and there was something about him being unlovable to most that made me feel like he was exactly the opposite. But with Apollo, the attraction had been immediate. Our souls had connected in a way that had had nothing to do with sex.

I couldn't explain that to Heracles. Even the demigod would think I was crazy, and he understood the gods and their antics.

"Tell me how the fight went," Heracles said, changing the

topic, and I was relieved. I talked to him about technique, about the power I had used to fight with, about my weapons and what had worked. The conversation became more comfortable as we slipped into our usual rhythm.

When my coffee was finished, I stood. "Thanks for hearing me out."

"Sure," Heracles said, refilling his cup with coffee, adding sugar and milk. "Anytime. I'm here for you."

"You can go back to bed now," I teased, sliding off my stool at the kitchen island.

"After I had coffee? Not a chance. I'll probably go for a run, so you want to come with me?"

I shook my head. "Thanks, but I haven't slept yet."

Heracles nodded and let me out.

The conversation with Heracles had been good in a way, the weight on my shoulders fading. He hadn't judged me and had instead made me feel normal, despite my attraction to the two gods. I wasn't like the rest of the humans. I had always known I was different. I could never completely relate to them, and I had made my peace with that a long time ago. But I was even more divided from them than I'd thought.

I was drawn to the gods, making me wonder if any of my ancestors had encountered deities and how they'd dealt with the magnetism. Or was it only happening to me? There was no denying that. I hadn't had contact with any of the others aside from Apollo and Hades, but it was safer for me to assume I would be attracted to the others if I ever ran into them too. Then, at least, it wouldn't catch me off-guard.

That still didn't change that it made me feel like I was at a disadvantage.

When I got home, I stripped off my battle clothes. I'd left my weapons behind, so I would have to get new ones, but it had been worth the sacrifice not to end up in bed—or somewhere sexy—with Hades again.

I climbed into the shower and stood under the hot spray, mulling over what I felt, over what Heracles had said. Even though he was a demigod, and I could ask him more about this, I couldn't tell him the full story.

I had no one I could talk to about this.

By the time I had dried my hair and crawled into bed, I was exhausted, but sleep wouldn't come. I was worried about what was happening to me, worried about how this seductive dance with the gods and me would affect me going forward. How could I fight if I was a lover?

I thought about what Heracles had said again. I was a lot less human than I had thought. I was a mortal but barely. I was powerful, but I was not a god.

But if I could overcome the human weaknesses to become a warrior who could fight supernatural warriors, surely I could overcome my other weaknesses, too. Love was a weakness, was it not? Physical attraction crippled so many of the people around me. So many of the women I knew had been hurt because they'd been drawn to deep eyes or a handsome smile.

I wasn't like the other humans. I was more like the gods. And if I could be like the gods in power, then I could be like them when it came to sex. If I overcame my human side to fight and defeat adversities that Death himself threw at me, I could overcome this too.

I was mortal, but who said I had to be weak?

CHAPTER 15

Apollo

I should have stayed away from her. Elyse was nothing but trouble for me. If I acted on what I felt for her, I was going to get my ass kicked right back to Mount Olympus, where Zeus would make me be a god again, complete with the shiny little halo and the wine that everyone sipped so damn self-righteously. I cringed.

No, thank you. I was more of a whiskey man. And I wanted to stay here on Earth, where I had freedom to do as I pleased.

Which meant I was a complete idiot even considering going over to Elyse's place this morning. Yet still, I climbed on my bike, switched on the engine, and drove toward the magic that drew me. Called to me. Clawed at my insides to hurry.

That was the problem. There was something about Elyse I couldn't stay away from. She'd been on my mind since I'd first bumped into her, and I'd found myself needing her company. I couldn't explain the desire burrowing through me. When I was with her, I felt as if I had been underwater my whole life, and I could finally break through the surface and breathe.

If that wasn't poetic enough for the god of music and poetry, I didn't know what was.

The whole thing pissed me off—how I felt this way about her—but I couldn't help myself. And staying away from her only caused me pain. The kind that tore at my chest like a blade-wielding maniac using me as target practice.

As I drove, the sun broke through the clouds.

"I haven't seen you in a while," I said to the sunshine, my chest beaming, a smile splitting my mouth. "Many a bright mornings I have seen, but none compared to the brightness in her celestial eyes."

What a beautiful sky. Everything looked better when it was illuminated by the shafts of gold that fell from the sky. I couldn't wait to see Elyse.

Except she wasn't home when I arrived. Good. I could turn around and return to my place. Stop being an ass and live the life I had chosen here on Earth, away from the gods and their bullshit. And falling head over heels for a human, let alone a Lowe, had not been part of the deal. Maybe I ought to leave the city. I'd only just arrived in Chicago from traveling the country, and already I regretted my decision to come here.

I got back onto my bike as Elyse's car pulled into a parking spot along the street, and she climbed out. My pulse sped at her presence.

She eyed me warily. She wore yoga pants and a matching black top, hair sticking out of her braid, her cheeks blushing red as if she'd been running a marathon, and clothes hanging off her.

"What are you doing here?" She frowned, her eyes

avoiding mine as if meeting my gaze made her admit her true feelings.

I didn't know how to answer that. I longed to be around her, to bask in the warmth I had felt when we shared time together. Even if only for a short period. But it wasn't enough, and I needed to get to know her, make her laugh, discover her favorite meals, if she loved theater.

"I came to see you." My words rolled out huskily past my lips as I leaned forward on my bike.

"I'm not in the best mood today. But thanks for coming over."

She edged past me, and the moment she did, her magic leaped out and stroked me as it had the last time we'd met. My cock twitched in my pants, and I pictured her under me. Or on top of me. Whichever was more fun. Her breath caught in her throat. She felt it too. I climbed off the bike and moved toward her, lightning fast, and I was suddenly so close to her, her floral shampoo she used swimming on the breeze. Uncertainty clung to her, and I intended to drive it away.

"Whatever you're feeling, don't fight it," I said, lifting my hand and hooking a lock of stray hair that had escaped from her braid behind her ear. She looked up at me. My dick strained against my jeans. A hunger roared through me, and I could smell her excited scent. She was as aroused as I was. I ran my thumb along her lower lip, my palm on her cheek, and she closed her eyes and sighed, leaning into my hand.

In all the years I'd lived on Earth, I hadn't kissed anyone. It was a rule I had made for myself not to get attached, and it had worked. But this was Elyse... She was a weakness I had not prepared for. I couldn't help myself. We stared at each other, and I studied her beauty as her hands gripped my arms like a lifeline. Rich, mocha eyes that stole my breath, the small freckles on her nose, and her pouty lips...oh, I needed to taste that mouth. I leaned down, dipping my head to reach her small frame, and kissed her. Close-mouthed at first, but she parted her lips and welcomed me. Our breathy kiss was like riding my bike at full speed at dusk, the cool breeze whistling through my hair, cooling me, reminding me how incredible life was. I grasped her tight, adoring the way her body melted against mine.

The moment she did, our powers flared up and wrapped around each other. Heat rolled over me in waves, shaking me. This was what I had been looking for. This was what had been missing all these years—for someone to affect me this way, for our energies to connect. I'd heard tales of knowing when you met that one person who would steal your heart in an instant—giving you no choice in the matter. Was this what I felt?

"Can I come inside with you?" I asked, my voice deepening.

Elyse swallowed hard and nodded, her eyes never leaving mine.

The power was hesitant to let us step away from each other. But we managed, walking to her front door together. She fiddled with unlocking the door as I reached out, touching her shoulder, then we headed inside.

The door was barely shut when I pressed her against the wall. I cupped her breast with one hand, bending my knees and closing her between my thighs so that I could grind against her. She was so much smaller than I was; I didn't exactly reach her crotch as much as her stomach, but the more I ground against her, the more her arousal spiked, her scent floral and delicious in my nose.

And our magic agreed. Our powers intertwined until I couldn't tell whose was whose. I didn't care, either. Electricity flowed from her body to mine and back.

"You're spectacular," I said. "I plan to show you the world, the beauty hidden on this planet and beyond."

Elyse's gentle smile encouraged me to reach for her shirt and tug it up. Under her top, she wore a sports bra. Women liked wearing the lacy, pushup shit, but this was fantastic on her. I cupped her breasts with both hands and kneaded them, kissing Elyse again.

She moaned into my mouth. "I missed you."

"Me too." Fire roared through my chest at hearing those words, unable to get enough of her.

I picked her up, Elyse wrapping her legs around my waist, then I carried her to the only bedroom I could find. It had a double bed, and I laid her down on it. She looked at me with hunger-filled eyes.

"When I'm with you, I feel like I've found myself," she said. "And I want more."

My emotions exactly.

I climbed onto the bed and straddled her, my legs on either side of her waist, pinning her down. She ran her hands up and down my thighs.

I reached for her braid and pulled the elastic free. Dark strands spread on the bed around her like a halo. She continued to run her hands up and down my legs, inching closer and closer to my groin.

"You'll be the end of me," I growled, then dove to her mouth again, sliding my tongue between her lips, tasting her, letting myself drown. This was what I'd missed for all these years...the connection a kiss brought. Her groans. The wickedness of her tongue teasing mine.

Several minutes later, I shifted off her and drew her pants and panties down. She gnawed on her lower lip, and the innocence drove me insane. Her legs were long and smooth, her body sculpted like that of a goddess. I had fucked her before, but I hadn't seen her naked, and by the gods, she was divine.

I wanted her completely naked so I moved to her bra, but

I didn't know how to take it off. Bras were tricky for a god who had been used to simply-tied fabrics, and most girls on Earth stripped for me. This padded shit was beyond me.

Elyse giggled and helped me with the bra, sitting up and undoing it behind her back, pulling it down her arms. "I'm surprised you struggled with the clasp."

But my focus was on her perfect breasts, which jiggled as she moved her arms. They were swells of perfection, her dark nipples tight.

Gently, I pushed her back so she lay down on the bed, and I climbed back onto her. I was in control. I ran my fingers through her long, chocolate hair. The stuff was like silk. I kissed her on the lips, unable to get enough of her sweetness, guessing I could lie next to her for eternity and just kiss that perfect mouth. But I moved down her neck and onto her chest. When I sucked a nipple into my mouth, Elyse and I moaned at the same time. I had been with many women, but Elyse tasted like nothing I'd ever had before. Her skin was almost orgasmic, and my cock throbbed.

I had wanted all of this the last time. Spinning her around and fucking her from behind had been the best way I could keep myself in check. I had yearned to rip her clothes off and make her mine right there that day but had resisted, fearing I'd fall for her. Well, I'd been kidding myself. Whatever was going on between us was more intense than anything I'd experienced before, and it was a fucking irresistible force that grabbed me by the balls and refused to release.

All of that was out of the window now. I was playing with fire, and I was begging to get burned. Because this feeling of her magic licking my skin, leaving a searing sensation in its wake, wasn't only orgasmic, it was addictive.

My fingers were still in her hair, unable to get enough of the stuff. I pinched her nipple with my mouth and massaged her other breast with my free hand.

I moved down her body, shifting on the bed as I did. The mattress creaked with the strain under my body. Elyse wove her hands into my hair. I loved the feel of her fingers on my scalp.

I kissed my way down over her abs, toward the V between her legs. When I kissed her pussy, Elyse gasped. I slid my tongue between her lips and flicked her clit with my tongue. She writhed under my hands, moving her hips against my mouth. She tasted like honey, like the nectar of the gods. I growled against her, which made her groan again. I could listen to those sounds all day.

Slowly, I licked her, tracing circles and figure eights over her clit, doing to her what I had learned from so many women. But it was different with her. I didn't know what it was, but with Elyse, it felt as if this was what I had been working toward my whole life—what I'd been waiting for.

I pushed a finger into her, and she was tight, her body clamping down on my digit. She was so fucking wet, I wanted to mount her and ride her hard and fast, but I was going to take my time. I was already past the point of no return. If this was the woman who would get me sent back to Mount Olympus, I was going to enjoy every second of it.

She moaned again when I added another finger and started moving in and out of her. I sucked on her clit, closing my lips, and Elyse cried out. I finger-fucked her harder and faster, and she squirmed, closing her hands into fists in my hair, tugging at it. It drove me crazy with lust.

When she fell apart, climaxing, screaming, I groaned against her pussy, and I knew she could feel the sound. Her body pulsated, drawing my fingers deeper into her, and her power washed over me so that I shuddered with her. The energy that washed over me tugged at my arousal, and suddenly, I released. My dick twitched and jerked, leaking into my pants, and I groaned as my muscles bulged.

I let go of her to recover as she writhed on the bed in ecstasy. I needed to recover too. I had no idea what the fuck that was, but I needed more of it.

Elyse was breathing hard, limp on the bed. Her lids were drooped, and she offered me a satiated smile. "That was incredible."

"It's only the beginning." I drew her into my arms, and she fit perfectly. Both of us lay there on the bed, and if I could have frozen time, I'd have done it then, with the two of us forever locked in place together.

"Tomorrow I want to take you for breakfast at a great place I found that overlooks the sea," I whispered.

She twisted her head around to face me, smiling. "Whatever's going on between us, I want it to be real."

"Sweetheart." I leaned closer and pressed my lips to hers. "I've never felt anything this powerful before. Never been attracted to anyone this way. This is real."

She kissed me again, faster and intense.

I wasn't done with her. Judging by the scent of her arousal, she wasn't, either.

But another smell had joined hers. It was a spicy musk. I had never sensed it when I had been with women before, but I knew instinctively that this smell belonged to me. It was the scent of my own arousal, of the claim I was trying to lay on her, and I couldn't help it.

Elyse propped herself up on her elbows, staring at me with the sexiest eyes.

"This won't do," she said, tugging my shirt up. I took over, dragging it off. She would have to stand to pull it over my head. I dropped it on the floor, and Elyse's gaze roamed my body. I knew I was built well. All the gods were. My abs were perfectly proportioned, my pectorals bulged, my arms stretched the shirts I wore to the limit. My jeans strained around my thighs. We were sexual beings with perfect bodies that exuded desire with one look. I saw the hunger grow as Elyse stared at me.

She reached for my buckle and undid my pants. When she reached into my pants and wrapped her fingers around my hardness, I exhaled loudly. Scalding heat followed, rolling off her in waves, and I let it flow over me.

Elyse looked up at me, her hand on my dick, which was hard and thick, throbbing, slick with the aftermath of my unexpected orgasm. Elyse looked surprised, her eyes widening, and smirked.

"You came," she teased.

"You are my undoing."

"Poetic," she replied, blowing me a kiss.

I wanted to respond, to say something blasé, to blow it off. But Elyse leaned forward and sucked the tip of my cock into her mouth, and I forgot how to speak.

She sank down on my dick, taking in as much as she could. She couldn't get me all the way without pushing into her throat, but I didn't care. Her mouth was like fire, and if I hadn't just orgasmed, I would have released in her mouth.

I let her bob her head up and down a few times, but the more she worked her mouth over me, meeting her lips with her hands where she couldn't take it all in, the more I wanted to be inside of her. I needed to fuck her.

When I threaded my hands into her hair, Elyse stopped sucking me off and looked up at me.

"You're beautiful," I said. "And all mine."

She looked as surprised as I was at the words that had fallen out of my mouth. I leaned down and kissed her again before I could say anything else that was stupid. In haste, I grabbed a rubber from my jeans and strapped myself. Then I flipped her over and drove her backward, spreading her legs with my knee, and positioned myself at her entrance. Elyse gasped against my lips when I thrust into her. Her gasp turned into a moan as I worked my way in. She was so tight and so hot, her body grabbing me and pulling me deeper.

When I was buried inside of her, I drew back. I fucked her, sliding in and out slowly at first, teasing her. But I tormented myself too.

She cried out as I rode her, and I looked her in the eyes when they were open. When she closed them, I watched her face as her mouth rounded in an O, her long lashes fluttering on her cheeks, and her skin becoming flush as she neared another orgasm.

When she came again, her pussy clung to my dick, and I stopped moving. I was going to release again if I wasn't careful. I could keep orgasming again and again because of her and stay erect. It was the joy of being a god. But if we came together, I didn't know what would happen. We were already drowning in magic.

Elyse opened her eyes, the orgasm subsiding, and she was panting. I grabbed her body, holding her by the hips, and rolled over. We nearly fell off the bed, but she ended up on top of me. She broke into laughter, and I joined her. Her hair fell over her shoulders when she leaned forward, the strands brushing my chest. I tangled my hands in it and pulled Elyse down to kiss me again.

She moved her hips while our lips were locked, and I growled against her lips. She moaned softly in time with the rhythm as she stroked faster, sliding my dick in and out of her. I let go of her hair and put my hands on her body. I could feel her muscles under her skin. There wasn't much fat on her. She could have been an immortal. Her looks, her magic, it was all there.

Elyse closed her eyes and pressed her hands on my chest as she rocked harder and harder. Her breathing became shallow, and I knew she was getting close to another orgasm. I was getting there too. I couldn't help it. Her breasts jiggled above me, her hair brushed my chest, and her pussy was so fucking tight.

When she came again, I couldn't help myself. Elyse's body contracted, milking my dick, and I released inside of her. Or inside of the condom. I hated wearing it—they were so fucking restricting. But I had to make sure she didn't end up pregnant.

Exploding together created a meltdown as my body buzzed all over, the world shaking. Our magic exploded all around us, and we were somewhere else. Not on Earth. I couldn't focus on my surroundings, but Elyse took me to another plane of existence. We cried out, moaning and rocking together. I wrapped my arms around her and pressed her against me, and we rode out the waves of power and pleasure together until I had no idea what I was going to do without her.

When the power subsided, Elyse's eyes stayed closed.

"Elyse," I said in a low voice, but her body was limp on mine. Carefully, I lifted her off me and rolled her onto the bed. I knew she was okay, her breathing steady, heavy as if she'd fallen into a sleep. Her magic was still surrounding us, brushing up against me, soft and gentle now. The energy had knocked her out. It was a strong reminder that she was a mortal.

And I was in huge shit for going there with her. Zeus would come for me. *Fuck!*

Carefully, I climbed off the bed. I got cleaned up and dressed fast. I made sure Elyse was covered, made sure her apartment was secure, and left her to have the best sleep of her life. Her body was drained from the magic, and she needed to recuperate. I needed fresh air, to clear my head, and maybe not be here when she woke up because we'd continue having sex. And then what? Me getting banished back to Mount Olympus, grieving for Elyse? Gods fell in love quick, no doubt, but how fast she was growing on me scared me. Except now, I wasn't sure I could walk away... and I'd promised her breakfast.

When I stepped out of the apartment building, my nerves a tangle of anxiety, Hades stood in the road. I halted, my pulse racing.

"What do you want?" I asked.

"What were you doing in there?" he asked, his voice distant. He didn't quite sound like himself.

"That's none of your business," I snarled.

Hades face twisted into a frown. He was angry. Or upset. Or something. He trembled lightly, and a cloud of darkness surrounded him. It was late in the day—Elyse and I had been at it for quite some time—but the clouds that covered the skies were so dark, it seemed almost like night. Hades was royally pissed off.

"What are you doing here?" I asked.

"You fucked her," Hades said in low voice.

"I didn't realize she's off-limits," I said. "What are you going to do about it?"

Hades trembled. His hands were balled into fists, and the darkness grew thicker. He was pissed off about this, but fuck him.

"Do you have a thing for her?" I asked, surprised. Everyone knew Hades wasn't capable of love unless it was a spell. Persephone was the result of that. But they had separated, or so I had heard.

"That's none of your business," Hades snapped, throwing my own words back at me. He turned around and evaporated. The light returned, the clouds dissipating as if the darkness had never been.

"What the hell was that about?" I frowned, not expecting Hades to care about anything. Definitely not about Elyse. Why was he here on Earth, bringing X with him?

Unless X was here for something else?

Could it be that Hades hadn't released X? Was there a different reason why X had broken free?

Maybe it had something to do with Elyse, which might have explained why Hades had come to see her.

CHAPTER 16

Elyse

*W*hen I woke up, darkness shrouded my vision at first. But the blinking clock on the nightstand told me it was nine o'clock at night. The day had not only been consumed by sleeping, but a delicious feeling crept over my body, and I curled in bed and smiled. I turned my head to the side, but the spot next to me was empty. I frowned and ran my hand over the sheets. Cold. Apollo had been gone awhile. Maybe he had never stayed. I couldn't remember going to bed together.

I rolled onto my back and sighed. I had hoped to wake up in his arms. But if I had to be honest with myself, how would that have worked out between us?

What I felt for him hadn't been just lust or a spell. Our time together wasn't about sex anymore, although that was still a big part of it. It was so much more. Even while my body thrummed with desire, beneath the surface I longed for his affection, his attention, his time. My skin still tingled from his touch, and my breath caught as I remembered being under him. My chest expanded with excitement, passion, desire to the point of explosion.

Apollo had an *I-don't-care* attitude. The first time we had connected together, he had fucked me from behind without kissing. It had been strangely impersonal. Maybe he'd taken me that way to avoid getting too close. Was he struggling with his emotions as well? The Apollo I had seen last was a very different god from the Apollo I had first met.

This god had been pure and kind and warm and loving. He was the kind of man I could fall desperately in love with. And just thinking those thoughts had my chest clenching because he affected me more than he should have.

I got out of bed, able to understand why Apollo had left. He was scared. What was the alternative? Play happy family, making breakfast together? Talking about a future like there could be one? He was a god, and I was a mortal. Yeah, I had power, and when we were together, our energies merged like they had been forged from the same enchantment. But we couldn't exactly go changing our Facebook statuses or anything.

When I walked to the bathroom, my thighs ached from last night. Apollo was a big boy—in every way—and the tenderness between my legs was of the fucking-fantastic variety. I stepped into the shower, and when the steam rose around me, the hot water pouring over my skin, the shower filled with the musky spice of Apollo's skin. I could still taste him on my tongue, feel his echo inside of me.

I smiled and couldn't help it. I must have looked like a lovesick teenager, but thinking about Apollo brought images of our time between the sheets to mind. Our bodies pressed against each other, Apollo's large frame covering mine, making me feel small and delicate. The way he was rough and gentle at the same time. The way he had taken me as if he had wanted to claim me.

And how I was okay with that at the moment? I couldn't say my sentiments had changed, but he was still Apollo, god of poetry and music, god of the sun. And I was a human. Yes, I was a Lowe, but I was everything but immortal or a god. Years after I perished, Apollo would live on, fucking other women.

Those thoughts drained the warmth and happiness from my body. I didn't want to think about such things because I couldn't see a solution any which way I looked at the situation.

"God, snap back to reality, Elyse." I had to be honest with myself and admit that a relationship with Apollo wasn't going to happen. Yet my chest ached at the thought.

I shook my head. I had to stop thinking about it, about what we had done. Nothing could come of our attraction.

After showering and drying my hair, it was almost midnight, and my routine was officially messed up. I walked to the kitchen to make something to eat.

I opened the fridge and stared at the leftovers. A sandwich would be perfect, so after making myself a PB&J, I walked into the living room. When I switched on the television, I found only the news was playing on every channel, I frowned.

Ten people had collapsed in town today, all of them dead with no explanation. Ten of them. The bodies had been taken to the morgue, but I knew they would never get autopsied. They would turn to dust and disappear.

I knew exactly what had happened to them. This was the work of X, which meant Hades was to blame for this because he hadn't stopped him. What the fuck was he doing?

I put the sandwich down after taking only one bite, but I had lost my appetite. What a buzzkill. After I'd had a wonderful day with Apollo, this was the kind of news I didn't need.

I still couldn't believe Hades would allow humans to die and X to lose control. He was the god of the Underworld, not of death. And the person I had gotten carried away with that first time had been sexy and likeable. Even when we had been fighting, when I had been furious with him for letting me win, Hades had been constantly on my mind, completely and wholly. The sexual tension had ramped up between us toward the end, and I had nearly given in.

The moment I thought about Hades and our sexual attraction, I felt guilty. I had run away from Hades because I hadn't been able to handle where our relationship was going. Then I had come home and slept with Apollo. What did that say about me?

Heracles had told me the gods didn't see sex the same way humans did. They didn't get emotionally involved. But I hadn't been able to tell Heracles this was different. I couldn't tell him emotions stirred within me for two gods. After I'd been with Apollo, I knew it wasn't one-sided, either. At least not with him. Maybe it was one-sided with Hades. Our power had recognized each other, and there had been something there.

I was sure of it. There was a side of Hades that drew me. I'd felt evil in X. Yet there was nothing about Hades that was like that.

The images on the TV changed, drawing my attention again, and I watched as they showed the scene of the incident near The Bean sculpture at Millennium Park. There were police everywhere, but in the background, amidst the crowds, I spotted Hades. "What the hell?" I leaned closer, squinting at the bystanders. He was on camera, looking like a regular human to the rest of them, but I knew him. He couldn't hide from me.

What bothered me most was the expression on his face. He had his arms crossed over his chest, his brows pulled together in a slight frown, but the overwhelming feeling that I got was that he was bored.

How could he be so blasé about death, about people dying?

Had I been wrong about him? Was he on Earth to cause mass destruction? Heracles had warned me Hades would make trouble.

I curled my hands in my lap, my pulse racing. *Fuck!* I actually cared about Hades, no denying it, even if I didn't want to. I had hoped he would be a hero of some kind, not a villain.

But heroes didn't look bored when they watched death and destruction.

The more I thought about it, the more riled up I grew, and I sucked in short, sharp breaths. I was born to fight, born to protect people. Right now, innocents were being harmed, and I was going to make sure they were avenged. I couldn't save the ones already dead, but I could do something about the rest. X was number one on my list of villains to defeat. Hades was the next.

I left my sandwich on the coffee table and marched back to my room, getting dressed for battle. Lately, it felt like I was either dressed up in my leathers and weapons or I was naked. I pushed the thought away. Why had I been naked? I didn't want to think about Apollo.

I drove down to the Millennium Park to where the murders had taken place and parked a couple of blocks away. The press were still milling around everywhere, with police officers and ambulances lighting up the area with red and blue flashing lights.

X had to be here somewhere. Killers loved watching the aftermath of their atrocities. So why wasn't Hades doing anything to stop the monster? Or was he involved? I cringed on the inside, my gut hurting, not wanting to believe that.

There were hundreds of souls to harvest tonight if he went on a killing spree. X wouldn't... would he?

I couldn't track him with all the flashing lights and people running around trying to make a difference with something that was already too far gone. I could feel him, though. It was subtle, nothing more than a shiver that ran down my spine, but it was enough to go by.

Eyes shut, I focused on that sensation. The chill of Death made the hair on my neck stand on end, and I tasted bile in my throat. I was terrified, no denying it. X was stronger than any god I had ever fought. He was pure evil. A small voice in the back of my mind shouted that I was running to my death if I was going to look him up. But I ignored the fear. The power around me rose, swelling, pressing, suffocating, and I knew, as I moved away from the people and toward the darkness, that I was on the right track.

But there was something else in the air tonight...something I couldn't explain. Fear hung heavily in the night, looping around me, invading my mind. But this wasn't me... it was someone else's terror. Not the bystanders near the crime scene because this felt different. It curled over my skin like snakes, my focus changing to a carousel of thoughts about fighting to the end. Rage bubbling in my chest, my breath racing, muscles ready. All I felt was fury in that moment for the lost lives.

Revenge.

Nothing would stop me.

The power intensified as I moved closer, the air thickening. The terror became so strong, my legs moved faster. My own thoughts started to fade, the promise of facing Death propelling me forward. I was the only one who could stop this. If I didn't, no one would.

"What are you doing here?" Hades barked, stepping in front of me from a crowd of people.

Startled at first, I froze on the cemented path before pushing ahead. "Get out of my way."

Hades put his hand on my shoulder, stopping me. His power licked me like a giant tongue and revived my magic where it had been gasping for air, breaking through my power.

"You should leave," he demanded, people brushing past us as if not noticing we stood there.

"Why? So you can allow X to kill again?"

"What are you talking about?" Hades growled, his brow creasing into a dozen lines. He was pissed, but I wasn't going to leave, no matter how scary he could be. What he and X were doing was deadlier. Rage churned within, starved for destruction, the pressure a raging sea forcing me to say things, yelling for me to shove Hades aside.

"The ten people who died here. Or is it so run-of-the-mill for you that you need to be reminded of the souls that were lost?"

Hades shook his head. "I'm not part of that."

"Sure you're not," I snapped, remembering his facial expression on the television. "Now let me pass."

I stepped forward, and my energy surged to challenge Hades's if he pressed the matter. But at the same time, his power was a relief. It felt as if I could breathe again as my sexual arousal surged within. Approaching and focusing on X had accelerated my energy in a way that drove my adrenaline to rage while Hades's power soothed me. But I had to stop the fiend before anyone else died.

"You can't beat him," Hades declared, his voice matter-of-fact, as if I were a child who didn't know any better.

"Because he won't let me win like you will?" I asked. "You should be encouraging me to fight him. Another death to take credit for."

His faced reddened, his eyes narrowing. I sensed his rage

flare, the scalding heat from the river of lava now palpable right here on Earth.

But I was as pissed off as he was. He snatched my wrist and drew me near the building and away from the flow of people.

"This isn't my fault," he snarled. "I didn't kill them."

"No, X did. But who brought him here, Hades?"

"I don't know!" he shouted, and I was taken aback for a second. Hades took a deep breath. "I don't know what the fuck he's doing here. I sure as shit didn't invite the guy. I may be the ruler of the Underworld, but Death is piss-poor company to keep, let me tell you that."

I paused for a moment. If Hades had no idea how X had come, then he wasn't the villain after all. Or was he lying to me?

"Fine," I said, shrugging as if his admittance didn't affect me or remind me that I didn't have to challenge him again. "I'll scratch you off my dance card for tonight, but I'm taking X on if you aren't going to help me, and you can't stop me." And with the last word leaving my mouth, the surge of fiery anger that came from X flowed through me once again, smoldering underneath my skin.

"Wanna bet?" Hades growled, his shoulders curling forward as he readied to manhandle me. He was determined, his black eyes steely. I wasn't in the mood for his games. Any other day would have been fine, but if I couldn't do the one thing I had been put on this Earth for, my existence was pointless.

"I'm going to fight him one way or another," I hissed. "Especially if you're not going to do anything about his murderous rampages."

"It's not that simple," he insisted. "I'm not letting you battle him because you won't win. I need to time to work out how to deal with him. So stop being so stubborn. Please. But if you insist on acting out with X instead of using your logic, you'll have to get through me first." His voice wavered as if saying the words shattered him. Something swam behind his gaze, a dreadful fear that I'd never seen on him before. What scared him so much?

Except he was stopping me from doing my job. From saving innocents. He was a god and should be fighting to stop X alongside me, not pushing me aside. Except that surge of fury that came from X slammed into me again. Nothing but blinding wrath throttled me, as if I'd lost control of everything. He brought out a primal anger in me. But that didn't matter as it only made me stronger to stop X. My face burned, my fists clenched. I rolled my eyes, shaking off the shiver clinging to my flesh. What the hell was going on with me? What was X doing to me? Yet I couldn't stop myself or the urgency to fight X as if he called to me.

The wave of powerful energy struck again, and that time, I only saw red.

"Fine. If you want your ass kicked, I'm ready." I drew my sword from the sheath on my back and brought it down straight, aiming for Hades's face.

CHAPTER 17

Apollo

I didn't want to lose Elyse. Except something fucked-up was going down. Energy clamped around me, and I expected Zeus to come claim me any second now and toss me back into Mount Olympus. What could I possibly say to make him reconsider?

Grinding my teeth, I set down the now-empty shot glass on the bar. I sat on my stool, with no strength to move. Zeus would never let me return to Earth again—at least for a millennia. How in the world would I say goodbye to Elyse? I crumpled the napkin I'd been scribbling a poem on for her. But I could barely string two words together.

Every inch of me longed for her, but then what?

I'd failed and given in because I hadn't been able to ignore the way my heart pounded each time I thought of her.

And I was royally fucked because the magic pressing down on me had to be Zeus coming. The supernatural shockwaves that pulsated through the air…

141

Maybe I ought to move to another country as far from her as possible.

I flagged down the bartender and downed a few more shots of whiskey, expecting to find Zeus thundering through the roof into the bar. But with each drink, time stretched out and no god. Alcohol took a lot longer to take effect in my body, but maybe I was starting to get tipsy by jumping to conclusions. Perhaps the energies were from something else in the surrounding city, and I had to find out what was going on rather than sitting here and feeling sorry for myself.

Outside, I flagged down a cab and pointed in a direction where the heat waves were strongest.

"Keep heading west," I said.

"Until when?" he asked.

"Until I say stop." I pulled out a wad of cash. Cash was a language every human on Earth spoke.

The closer we got to the city center, the stronger the shockwave became until it shook me like an earthquake with every pulse. The driver felt nothing. None of the humans would. He sang along to the radio as he drove, blissfully unaware that the world might very well be ending.

What the hell was going on tonight?

"Here is fine," I barked as my body vibrated from the sensation. I threw the wad of cash at the driver, jumping out of the car before it came to a full stop. I hit the road at a dead run toward some kind of park, going for the source of the power that rocked through me.

I skidded to a halt when I finally saw her. Elyse was wielding a sword, and she was in a fight with Hades. This was where the magic was coming from?

Elyse was powerful. Stronger than she had ever been, than any Lowe had been. The magic that pulsated through the air was so thick, it pushed into my throat, my lungs, with every breath. I tasted her on my tongue, felt her in my veins, and my heart shuddered.

Hades was fighting as if this was serious. He had that fucking pitchfork with him, the two-pronged bitch that obliterated anything that wasn't a god, and he was swinging his weapon over his head. If he managed to get past Elyse's power and her sword, he could kill her. I tensed, my muscles flexed, my hands curled into balls.

The pitchfork grazed her shoulder, and she stumbled backward, her breath hitching. She dodged another attack and ducked, stabbing at Hades's leg, but he jumped out of reach. Hades was going to kill her if they didn't stop this shit. After he had seen me coming out of her apartment earlier in the day, he looked ready to explode after finding out Elyse and I had had sex.

I charged toward them. Elyse needed my help. I had to stand up for her, defend her. She was the one woman I had risked everything for. I couldn't stand by and do nothing.

When I raced closer, Hades pinned me with his eyes that held no anger or hatred. His gaze was full of pleading, like he was afraid. I halted in my tracks. What did Hades have to be terrified of if he was fear itself?

Hades looked over his shoulder for a second, but it was enough to tell me what was going on. The power that I felt wasn't from a brawl. It was an intervention. Hades stopping Elyse from something?

She fought with a fury that made her sexy as hell and likely to win this round if she kept it up. What was Hades keeping her away from?

I skirted the duo, peering into the darkness that swallowed everything behind Hades. My scalp crawled with terror and bloodlust—not my own but that of a creature I hated. Death was back there in one of the shadowy alleys. A guttural laughter echoed from his direction. The bastard was enjoying the show, amused by Hades battling Elyse.

As soon as I realized what was going on, X glared at me from the eternal darkness, his eyes glowing with a fire that consumed souls.

The deaths. The news. The people he had killed. Elyse was here to avenge them. To confront X for the lives of the humans she had been empowered to protect.

If she got through Hades and fought X herself, she would die too. Elyse wouldn't come back to life to fight again and again until her lives were depleted, either. X would consume her, and she would know an eternity of emptiness, rather than the peace that had been promised to her family by Zeus.

Hades was protecting her.

My heart shredded.

I couldn't stand up for Elyse.

Hades was doing the right thing, and if anything, I ought to step by his side. Force her to end this. But I couldn't fight against her. Not in this lifetime or any. If I battled Hades, joining forces with Elyse, we would win. But that would lead to her demise.

Elyse would die at X's hands if Hades lost. She wouldn't come back from death at X's hands, but be gone for real. That was why we couldn't let her battle X.

Standing back hurt like hell, tearing me apart from the inside out, and I hated myself. But if I moved to her, I'd lose her for eternity. She'd perish from the world, and Hades's plan was the only way to protect her. This wasn't just about stopping Elyse today, but saving her the next time she attacked X. So I had to have faith this plan would work because she wasn't going to listen to us.

I sucked in a sharp breath, feeling as if someone had jammed a blade into my heart and twisted. My blood burned for her. Since meeting her, she'd been on my mind every second. Now my heart sank into the ground.

X crept closer.

Nausea churned unrestrained in my stomach, and regret formed in my head that if I'd stayed with Elyse, had returned to her place earlier, she'd be safe for now. Instead of facing Death, I could have brought her to unimaginable pleasures, holding her in my arms like we were meant to be. But such thoughts were useless, grating on my nerves, because if not today, tomorrow she'd attempt to battle Death. She wouldn't stop, so how was I meant to save her from herself?

Hades was right. She couldn't defeat him, yet I couldn't understand why she wasn't insistent on attacking X.

X moved like a shadow through the darkness; the only thing I could see of him was the black hair that blew like smoke in the wind and the eyes of ominous fire that threatened to devour the very thing that made Elyse so precious. Hades was standing in her way to keep her from reaching X, but no one was stopping X from getting to her.

I had to do something. If I couldn't help her from being who she believed she should be, I could help Hades save her.

CHAPTER 18

Elyse

I had never known such strength, such energy. When I brought my sword down, willing to slice Hades in two, hoping it was possible for me to destroy a god. It felt as if my power became infinite, rushing through me, firing up my nerves. I was suddenly hyper aware of my surroundings. Everything around me slowed down. My heartbeat banged in my ears, the time between each pulse stretching out into eternity. Beads of sweat trickled down my back, and I tasted the rage on my tongue. The anger grew hard and bitter, and I sucked on it, letting the fury fuel the energy I'd never known I possessed. This was unlike anything I'd ever experienced, and I savored the moment.

"X has to pay for what he's done," I shouted when Hades managed to deflect my blow, and I gritted my teeth against his strength, despite mine growing with intensity.

"You can't beat him," Hades repeated, his voice a growl.

"You will never think I'm good enough," I spat as I swung my sword at him again. Hades was fast on his feet, but I was quicker. I sliced his shoulder and darkness seeped out like water. The cut healed again in a moment. Hades was a god after all.

So how did I defeat a god who put himself back together over and over?

Heracles's teachings came back to me. There would always be a creature bigger than me, stronger than me, faster than me. I had to fight smart. But another pulse of energy overcame me, and with it came a wave of rage.

Fight.

Attack.

Nothing else mattered.

I would do that, and tonight, I had a new power on my side that I had never known before. My bitterness and rage fueled my magic. So what was I so upset about?

I hadn't been able to save the dead people, but instead, I had fallen for two gods who should have been on my side, and here I was battling one. I trembled with anger with myself for letting my feelings get in the way. Furious with Hades for not stopping X.

I was mad that he wouldn't let me pass to do what I had been born to do. He didn't see me as a worthy opponent or warrior who could take on the foe harming humans. But Zeus had picked my family for such situations. I was a warrior!

"You will die," Hades hissed, his eyes pleading with me, as if this hurt him. Gone was his condescending tone, replaced with terror in his gaze. Was he really afraid of losing me to X? Still, his change of heart touched me because I felt the good in people, and Hades wasn't bad. And seeing his fear amid the anger scared me too. But I couldn't let my emotions dictate my actions. My goal was straightforward: stop X at any cost. And Hades stood in the way of me completing my job.

"Thousands will die if I don't do this because no one else will stand against him." I pointed out.

"Just stop and listen to me," he insisted. "You can't survive this."

We were both breathing hard, our conversation punctuated by the sound of metal on metal as my sword and his pitchfork clashed again and again. But the wrath inside me rattled me at the core, burned me up, ignoring all rationality. But memories rose through me of my family killed in battle.

Dad!

I couldn't let him down. The fear of failing as he had, ate at me, so I threw myself at Hades, trembling in a frenzy.

Hades was pulling out all the stops, fighting a worthy battle, which meant I was a worthy opponent. I had trained long and hard for this. I ran miles every day. Heracles hammered attack techniques and weapons into my mind every morning.

Now I had the strength to back me.

Against all odds, I was winning.

I sensed Apollo before I saw him. His heat was like a giant hand at my back, the fog in my head clearing for a few moments. When I looked to the side, he was moving around us, walking toward Hades's back. He was going to aid me and attack Hades from behind. I beamed on the inside to have him here with me, to help me.

Apollo was a better ally. What I felt for Apollo was worth me falling for him. What did Hades make me feel? I didn't know what do with that emotion. Sure, my attraction to him was real—I wasn't going to fool myself. But Hades might turn out to be the bad guy despite his mixed signals. Had I been wrong earlier when I sensed the good in him? I couldn't be with the person who allowed souls to be taken before their time. I couldn't be with the villain if I was the last hero.

Hades took advantage of the moment I glanced at Apollo

and lifted his pitchfork over his head, his eyes on my chest. My heart thundered in my ears, and the darkness closed in around us. It was thick and heavy, worse than anything I had felt from Hades before. And my pulse raced with hatred for everything I'd lost in life.

"Apollo!" I shouted. "Help me!"

Apollo glanced toward me from within the shadows, but he didn't move or come to my rescue. He didn't attack Hades from behind. Our eyes locked, and in his, there was sorrow, an agony so great, it splintered my heart. He disappeared into the darkness within the blink of an eye. I grew hollow inside, raw, and more exposed than ever. The heartbreak struck me in waves, stealing my thoughts and strength. Where I'd felt whole moments earlier, now everything in me shattered, and only echoes of what I'd thought I had remained.

Apollo wasn't going to come for me.

Hades's pitchfork came down toward me, and I grabbed the blade of my sword with my free hand to block it. The edge cut my hand and blood ran down my arm.

A growl came from the darkness, and I could feel the thirst for my soul. X neared.

The pitchfork clashed against my sword, one prong on each side of the blade, and Hades drove it down as I pushed up, desperately trying to keep the sharp ends away from my heart. It cost all my strength. Hades had the power of the gods, the pitchfork that obliterated all who stood in Hades's way, and gravity was on his side.

All I had was my will. But now that Apollo had forsaken me, I was running out of steam. I had thought he loved me despite our short time together. Gods fell in love fast, and his tenderness and passion had convinced me of his intentions. I'd thought after the time we'd had that what I felt for him was mutual. But he had left without waking me, hadn't he?

And he was leaving again.

Another growl came from the darkness, and it drew me forward as if it were sucking my soul. Awakening the earlier rampage in my veins, blurring my thoughts... all except for the fear of losing. Somehow, I knew that on the other side of that darkness was an abyss, and if I fell into it, I would never return. I had no one on my side here to save me. I was as alone as I had been since losing my family.

My family was dead. Heracles didn't even know I was here in need of assistance, though he wouldn't be allowed to aid me. Apollo had forsaken me, and judging by Hades's frown, he had never been there for me in the first place.

I just wanted to get to X. I wanted to do the right thing. Wanted to save innocents. Not lose my heart and mind to reckless gods. But one thing I could rely on was the anger pivoting inside me, driving me with urgency to stop X.

To make up for losing my father.

To show him that if I had the chance, I could have saved him.

"He will kill you," Hades snarled, as if he knew what I was thinking. "Please, Elyse, listen to me!"

"And what are you doing?" I gasped, unable to speak properly under the strain of keeping the weapon away from me. Sorrow bled across his face, narrowing his eyes, pinching his lips.

The darkness crept ever closer, surrounding us. So thick, it was hard to breathe. I called to my power, but I was starting to fade while anger rose and fell through me as if two powers battled within me. My strength was weakening, returning to what it had been before. The stab of Apollo's betrayal siphoned my energy until I was only Elyse, the little Lowe who was one step away from being truly mortal.

I let out a battle cry and twisted the sword to the side. The pitchfork slid off, and Hades lost his balance, stumbling sideways. I rolled over and onto my knees, pushing up with the hand that held my sword while I cradled my injured hand to my chest. Blood poured out of it, soaking my sleeve, stinging to high hell. A deep gash covered my hand, the cut almost as black as Hades's healing injuries.

Yet the pain dulled to a numb sensation. A bad sign. Shallow injuries hurt like hell. A papercut was a bitch. But the bigger injuries, the ones that were life-threatening, didn't hurt until later.

I was in trouble and losing blood fast.

Hades recovered, and he came for me with his pitchfork, his face fierce and determined. I lifted my sword with wavering arms and deflected the prongs, but his staff knocked my temple, and the world tipped on its axis. For a moment, I saw stars as I fell to the ground a second time. My ears were ringing. Hades would kill me if I didn't get up.

The fact was a distant thought, my mind light and airy as if I were floating. I was superhuman in many ways, but I was fighting a god, and I wasn't immune to torture and injury.

I opened my eyes, and the world tilted beneath me. Stinging pain washed through my body in waves, and my stomach turned. I rolled onto my side so I didn't choke on my vomit if I threw up.

Why wasn't Hades attacking me? When I glanced up at him, I had tunnel vision. *Shit!*

Hades swam in and out of my sight. He was staring toward the darkness, his face anxious. Or was I dreaming? I struggled to separate rhyme and reason from the chaos surrounding me. Except for the heated rage burning through me.

I pushed myself up, every inch of me screaming with agony. Excruciating pain owned me and the nausea racked my body.

"Don't you ever stop?" Hades asked, and he sounded exasperated.

"Lowes don't quit," I said, thinking of the words my dad had taught me when I'd been a child. We fought to the death. It was the one thing that we always did. And I would do just that.

I limped toward Hades, my sword raised. I drove every ounce of power into the thrust and plunged the sword into Hades's side.

He cried out, a terrible roar that shook the foundations of the buildings around me. Outrage crossed his features, and when he looked at me, his eyes were completely black, the whites swallowed by pupils that had expanded to make him look like a demon, not the handsome man that I was attracted to.

An awful fury oozed from Hades's being. But when I looked at him, I couldn't stop seeing a man who had been rejected for all the horror he portrayed rather than being loved for all the goodness that he hid within.

"Snap out of it!" I screamed at myself. I had always thought that seeing the golden nugget of goodness in everyone was a gift. Tonight, it was a curse.

Hades's eyes morphed back to normal at the sound of my voice. Maybe he had thought I was talking to him. I ran toward him with my weapon drawn, ready to end this. Either Hades lost, or I did. Follow Dad's instructions, carry out our family mission. I couldn't let my dad down. Eliminate anything that harmed humans, that stood in our way. There was no other way this battle would end. I wasn't fighting Hades so much as I was attacking the villain I was trying to see him as. My heart had to stay out of the game because it would get me killed. I couldn't trust Hades, no matter how much my heart and my soul wanted me to.

Apollo stumbled out of the darkness. He looked terrible,

as if he hadn't eaten for months, breathing raggedly as if he'd run a marathon. His cheeks had grown hollow. His natural tanned skin had sunken in tone, and he had dark rings underneath his eyes. His once-golden hair was now dirty and clung to his face. He looked like he had been through hell and back; bruises and cuts littered his body, torn clothes hanging off him.

What had happened to him? I trembled, hating to see him this way. But those cerulean blue eyes were still his own, and they were locked on mine. Loving me. Calling to me.

"Please," I pleaded as Hades knocked me down once more.

I hit the pavement so hard, I thought I heard my bones clatter. Hades turned his head to look at Apollo, and something passed between them. Apollo shook his head slowly. I took the opportunity to push myself up again. If he wasn't going to support me, I would face this fucking battle myself. As soon as Hades was taken care of, X was next, and I was finishing this once and for all.

"Elyse, stop!" Hades shouted.

"Please, Elyse, listen to him," Apollo called out.

Fuck them both. No one stood up for me, and I was meant to back down? I stiffened, my throat thickening with agony, the sense of betrayal, being let down. He hadn't chosen my side. How could they stand in the way of me finishing X when the monster had killed people? I let out a shout and started toward Hades again. I wasn't as strong or as fast as I had been, but I still had fight left in me. Fire filled my veins to keep going, to make my dad proud.

"You're just an obstacle," I cried. "I'm not going to stop until I do what I came for."

"As long as you attack, I will as well," Hades hissed. He pulled back, winding himself up, and launched his pitchfork at me like a spear. He aimed for my left side, and I couldn't stop the pitchfork with the sword alone. My vision blurred, and my arm had started to go numb, the blood not clotting in the nasty cut on my hand.

The pitchfork hit me in the shoulder and dragged me backward, pinning me into the ground. I screamed with torment from the explosion of pain rattling through me. I was trapped.

Wriggling free was impossible, and it felt as if someone was hammering a stake into my shoulder over and over, the agony crushing through me all the way to my brain.

I released my sword and wrapped my fingers around the haft, but it didn't budge.

Hades stalked toward me. His eyes weren't the black they had been when he had been enraged, but they were empty all the same.

"I won't stop," I yelled in a hoarse voice, my eyes prickling from the stings wracking my body. But I blinked fast, refusing to show him any weakness. And in that moment, my head cleared of the haze. Why had I been so furious before instead of just talking to Hades to make sense of it all? My head spun, and I couldn't remember why I had been so angry.

"I know you won't," Hades said. He placed a hand on my chest and pulled the pitchfork out with his other. I twisted, crying in pain, but he held me in place, pinning me down, and my power evaporated from me. Spent, I fought to catch my breaths, to make sense of my messed-up emotions. I turned my head to Apollo. He stood at the edge of the darkness, his eyes filled with raw sorrow, his lips parted. But his hands hung by his side. He didn't start toward me.

I didn't ask him to help. I didn't reach for him. Apollo would not be my savior. I'd been a fool for believing he would be. My eyes prickled, but I blinked back the tears, the pinch in my chest, the burning inferno wearing me thin.

Hades lifted the pitchfork with the bloodstained prongs facing downward. It was all in slow motion as he pulled back, his form silhouetted against the night sky. For a change, the clouds had departed, and stars littered the sky, as if the gods had spilled their diamonds across the heavens. But they had no right being glorious. Not when my heart splintered, when I was about to lose a fight to Hades, when I shook as I stared at the sharp ends of his weapon. A cry bubbled on my throat.

"Hades, no!" I murmured.

But the pitchfork came down toward my chest.

"You'll live another day," Hades cried, but his voice was far away, as if I were hovering in a bubble. The prongs hit my chest, and I yelled out as they penetrated the flesh, cracked my ribs, and skewered my heart. My head fell to the side, and the last thing I saw was Apollo, turning his gaze away.

CHAPTER 19

Elyse

*W*hen I opened my eyes, I wasn't sure where I was. The light in the room was different. It was gray and dusky. I turned my head and realized I was in my bedroom.

My stomach clenched at my recent memory. Fuck! I had died.

Someone must have brought my body back to my apartment. Not Hades. He had killed me.

Apollo?

The moment I thought of him, a pang shot through my chest, and it was very similar to the pain of the pitchfork stabbing me in the heart. I shuddered, remembering the look on Hades's face, that pitchfork poised above my body, his hand like a thousand worlds weighing on my chest so I couldn't get up.

And he'd murdered me.

I did inventory on my body, patting myself. No part of me ached. I knew I'd had a concussion. I remembered my tunnel vision and the rolling nausea that had accompanied it. My head didn't hurt now. Instead, it felt light and airy, as if I had taken something super strong.

My shoulder didn't sting when I moved my left arm. Hades had pinned me to the ground with the pitchfork. The weapon had whistled through the air, and my body rattled through the vivid memory of the pain. I cringed, but that was all it was—a memory. Yet it sat on my mind like cement, weighed down on me, reminding me of my death. When I prodded my shoulder, nothing was wrong. There was no blood, no torn ligaments or ripped muscle. No broken bones.

My clothes were shredded, though. The black, long-sleeved shirt I always fought was torn. That was what happened when the god of the Underworld treated me like a pincushion. There were also two gaping holes in the material right over my heart in the material.

I'd fucking died.

I sat up and studied my left hand. No trace of the cut on my hand, self-inflicted when I had used my sword as a shield. Aside from the crusted blood on my sleeve and the holes and rips in my clothing, I was fine. My body had healed perfectly, as if the battle had never happened.

The feeling of death came back to me. Icy cold and dark. My throat closed, and my eyes flashed on Apollo's face, his lips pursed in a thin line, his eyes averted. My lover had watched me die.

And he hadn't given a shit. I'd been foolish to think any different. Fuck, just like all those lovesick humans in the myths who'd yearned for gods and gotten screwed in the end.

I pushed off the bed, and I felt surprisingly agile. Testing my theory, I lifted my legs, swung my arms, jogged on the spot. Everything was perfect.

I'd lost one of my lives. I could die twice more, and then

the final death would be my future. My father had talked to my brothers about what it was like to die…about the choking darkness that came back in waves now and then. He had mentioned it casually, as if it were no big deal, but you never really forgot what it was like to lose a life.

I wondered what the last time had been like for him. Warm, peaceful? That was how I had hoped it had been for him. But what if it had been as cold and dark as all the others? As the death I had experienced?

I stopped thinking about it or I'd drive myself crazy if I carried on like this. I had to focus on what was going to happen next.

I had no idea what that was.

Apollo was gone. So was Hades. One had abandoned me, and the other had killed me. There was nothing as final as death to end a relationship. If that was what it had been. Definitely, our time together had meant more to me than it had Apollo.

It would teach me not to get involved with the creatures I was supposed to battle. I was lucky I was still alive, but that was thanks to Zeus. I'd failed in keeping myself alive. I was the last fighting Lowe and pretty sure that wasn't going to last long if I carried on the way I had been. I couldn't rush into battle, but study my opponents, be smart, just as Heracles had said. Except that was all great in hindsight. At the time, I'd felt as if I'd had zero control of my flaring emotions.

Except something hadn't been right during the battle. The unyielding rage had taken me over, and making sense of things seemed impossible. I'd trained with Heracles for so long, and I knew to never blindly run into a fight, yet that was exactly what I'd done. I recalled the fury burning inside me, the need for the fight to the end, the agonizing need to not let my dad down.

And now when I thought back, that energy could only

have come from X. Apollo's and Hades's powers affected me sexually, but X wasn't exactly a god. He was Death, so what if he affected me differently? Just as he had the first time I'd met him after battling the centaur. *Fuck!*

So was I to blame as much as Hades when it came to how out of control things had gotten? Except he'd gone too far—there hadn't been a need to kill me.

Still, the hatred from X had engulfed me, driven me to act irrationally. The bastard had wanted me to fight him. And I felt beyond ready to destroy anyone in my way. Could my life get any more complicated?

When I stared at myself in the mirror, I looked surprisingly fit and healthy. My hair was a mess, my braid caked with blood, but my cheeks were flushed, my eyes were bright, and I was practically glowing.

Go figure.

I hopped in the shower to clean off the blood. I didn't want any extra reminders. The memories I kept flashing on were enough. When I stepped out of the water, another rush of cold washed over me, and I shuddered. Darkness descended on me, an echo of my death hammered through me as it had when I'd been stabbed through the heart.

How long was this going to last?

Someone knocked on my door, and I froze. Another bang sounded, and then Catina called my name.

I let out my held breath, dressed quickly in slim jeans and black tee, and hurried to the door, my hair still wet over my shoulders.

"Are you okay?" Catina asked, looking me up and down. She frowned slightly as if she somehow sensed what I'd gone through.

"I am," I replied, smiling. I'd only fought with one lover, had been deserted by another, had gotten killed, and then had come back from the dead. All in a day's work, right?

"Where were you?" Catina asked.

I blinked at her. I had no idea what she was talking about.

"The meeting you were supposed to have? For the photos?" She gripped her waist, glaring my way.

Shit. I had been fighting gods all week. I hadn't thought about work once.

"I told Tina you were sick. She was furious and ready to sack you. Tell me you were with your head in the toilet all day." She huffed a loud exhale as if needing me to placate her as well.

"Something like that," I said. Didn't being killed warrant a sick day?

Catina followed me back inside the apartment, and I closed the door.

"Are you sure you're okay?" she asked, her voice soft and caring.

"Why do you ask?" I headed into the kitchen to make coffee. I needed as much as I could humanly consume. I trembled, and I didn't know why. "Coffee?"

"Yeah. You're looking like you're miles away. What's going on?"

"Remember that guy I told you about?" I asked.

"The blond god who was a biker?" Catina stared at me as if expecting me to drop a bomb.

I froze and stared at her. What did she know about Apollo?

"That's how you described him," she said.

Right. "Yeah, that one. I think it's over between us." My mouth felt dry because this shouldn't affect me, but each word was a knife cutting deeper in my gut.

Catina pulled herself up onto the counter and leaned on her hands at the edge. I watched her knuckles turn white. It was such a small sign of life pumping through her veins, but I was fascinated by life, which was such a fragile thing, but it was so powerful at the same time.

"Was there anything to begin with? Apart from sex?" Catina's voice was still soft. "You didn't tell me."

"I thought there could be," I explained, pulling my gaze away from her hands and focusing on the coffee mugs I was preparing. This was instant coffee. Nowhere near as amazing as the coffee Heracles made, but I would take what I could get. "Guess I was wrong."

Catina was quiet for a moment, and the silence stretched between us.

"You were serious about him, weren't you?"

I shook my head, plastering a forced smile that felt wrong on my mouth. "Nah. You know me. I don't get serious about men." Which was totally true. It turned out that changed when it came to gods, though.

"Well, you'll find your Mr. Right one day. Until then, there're plenty of fish in the sea to keep you busy, right? You're amazing, Elyse. You'll find a great guy in no time."

I took a deep breath and blew it out slowly, nodding. The thing was, I didn't want all the fish in the sea. I didn't want the human men who courted me now that I'd had the most incredible experiences. It was like going back to bicycles after I had driven a sports car with a monster engine.

The whole idea of Mr. Right pissed me off. How was I supposed to know who he was if there was more than one?

What the hell was I saying? The two men—gods, whatever—both had been everything that could label them Mr. Right. Well, Apollo more than Hades. Then, they had fucked it up so righteously, I was pretty sure I was scarred for life. I guessed death could do that to a person.

"Hey, cheer up," Catina added when I finished making the coffee and turned to hand her a cup. "It's going to be okay."

Of course it was. I just didn't quite know the definition of "okay" anymore.

In the living room, Catina and I talked about trivial shit, work and deadlines, yet I couldn't tell her what had happened. So I let her ramble on about makeup and clothes and men and everything that felt so petty compared to what I was dealing with. I felt more removed from my life on Earth than ever. Catina was human, and I had always turned to her to remind me that I belonged here.

That sense of belonging was gone. I didn't feel like I belonged among the humans anymore. Seeing that I wasn't even close to being a goddess or anything like it, there wasn't anywhere else for me to belong.

When Catina finally left my apartment, I waved to her as she strolled down the stairs, and I was relieved. I wanted to be alone with my thoughts. I had to figure out what I was feeling. I needed to wrap my mind around what had happened, and I had to decide how I was going to move forward. I wasn't going to give up fighting for people here on Earth, but my enemies had increased when I had thought I had at least one of the gods on my side.

"Elyse," Oliver said, popping his head out of his door. "I'm glad I caught you."

I fought the urge to sigh. "How are you, Oliver?"

"I was about to ask you the same thing. I haven't seen you in a while. Are you working hard?"

"You could say that," I said.

Oliver came toward me, looking shy. When he opened his mouth, I knew he was going to ask me something. "How about a break from work? Come to dinner with me tonight." His words were strong and brave for a change. Good on him.

I shook my head. "I can't go out until the weekend."

Oliver frowned. "It's Friday."

Right. I had lost track of my days completely with my nocturnal—and then deceased—schedule.

I was about to say *no* to him, but Catina's words came back to me. Plenty of fish in the sea to keep me busy. A plus point about Oliver was that he was very human and there was no harm on going out to dinner. Maybe that was what I needed—more friends. To somehow be reminded how to be human again.

"Okay," I replied.

Here's to being normal.

CHAPTER 20

Elyse

I was getting ready to go out with Oliver. With my torn-up life, a bit of normality might be exactly what the doctor called for, to deal with everything I'd gone through lately. I had no clue how to process the last few days, let alone the ache in my chest each time I remembered Apollo and Hades, their sorrowful eyes before I'd died.

Aside from my training and fighting clothes, I owned mainly jeans and T-shirts in my wardrobe. I wasn't sure that would cut it for the dinner I knew Oliver had in mind. He'd been waiting for months to take me out. When I'd agreed, his reaction had been delayed, as if he'd expected me to say *no* again. I ought to have felt guiltier for finally saying *yes* this time, but my head was too confused to make sense. I yearned for time away from my mixed-up life.

I dove into my closet in my underwear and took out the only dress I owned. The black fabric hit me mid-thigh and pushed up my breasts way farther than I was comfortable with. But a sports bra wasn't the right thing for a date, and when I turned around, the dress made my ass look good. I hadn't ever tried to look sexy, but this wasn't bad.

What was I going to do with my hair? I usually braided it for training or fighting, but that seemed wrong too. So I let it hang loose. It hung over my shoulders. I still debated if I should leave it loose or not when a knock on my door announced Oliver was back for me. I'd expected some kind of tingle in my gut, but there was nothing there.

I still had to do my makeup, too.

"I'm almost done," I said when I opened the door, but Heracles stood before me, not Oliver. Startled, I lost my words at first, and instead emotions bubbled in my chest. Something about him, like he was a loving older brother, made me want to leap into his arms, cry, and have him tell me everything will be all right.

His gaze slid up and down my body, and he cocked an eyebrow. "Are you going somewhere?"

"Yeah," I said, pushing out a response. "Come in. I'm doing my makeup."

Heracles hesitated before coming into my apartment. In my room, he stared around at my empty space with minimal furnishings and decorations. Unlike his home.

I moved to the mirror and opted for neutral eyeshadow. Heracles sat down on my bed, and the mattress dipped under his weight. I glanced at him in the mirror.

"So, word has it you died yesterday," Heracles said without any emotion, but his mournful eyes gave him away.

"Yeah," I said, swallowing past the boulder in my throat, hiding the feeling that crept up my neck and cheeks.

"How are you feeling?" His voice dipped, smothered in concern, and for a moment, I expected him to stand up and embrace me.

I shrugged. "I don't know. How does it feel to come back from the dead? The only people I can ask are all dead for good. I will be too, soon. I guess it doesn't really matter." I stared down at the lipstick in my hand, my world sinking at how deflated I sounded.

Heracles frowned, his hands gripping the edge of the mattress on either side of him. "You're not abandoning the cause, are you?"

I laughed bitterly. "*The cause*. You say it like it's a thing."

"Don't be like this," Heracles insisted, reminding me of my dad when I'd tell him I didn't want the legacy. Didn't want to fight. Didn't want to spend my life battling supernatural creatures. "You can't give up."

I spun around, mascara on one eye and not the other.

"Easy for you to say. You're immortal, and you're not even a part of this fight. You're just the trainer. You don't exactly lay down your life for anything."

"Elyse, calm down," Heracles said.

I shook my head. "I'm not going to calm down. I died, Herc. Died. Do you know how? Or are the rumors a little vague in that department?"

"Hades only did it to save you," Heracles stated.

I forced a laughed, remembering Hades's pitchfork driven into my heart, him towering over me like some legend. Yeah, right. "What a fucking hero," I sneered.

Heracles shot to his feet and closed the distance between us. He put his hands on my arms, forcing me to stand still and look up at him. At the concern marring his brow, the shadows galloping under his eyes, the lines at the corners of his mouth as they tipped downward.

"You're doing so well, Elyse. Don't give up now. Everyone faces obstacles. Remember what the fates said. What defines you is how you decide to respond to hurdles."

"Sure. I'll keep going. I'll wait for every guy I fall for to betray me." I sounded bitter in my head, but I couldn't help it when every time I remembered a heartfelt moment with

Apollo, the tragic ending speared me in the chest over and over.

Heracles frowned. "You fell for Hades?"

"Apollo, actually," I said. "Or both. Who the fuck knows what's going on? I don't." I turned around to finish my makeup.

Heracles shook his head.

"Hello?" Oliver called from the open front door.

"Coming," I said. I walked over to him. Oliver was wearing a suit, and he offered me a broad grin when he saw me. When Heracles came out of my room behind me, Oliver's smile faded.

"Who's this?" he asked, his gaze tracing every inch of Heracles's enormous muscled frame.

"I'm her cousin," he said with a smile that didn't reach his eyes.

Oliver swallowed hard, looking intimidated, to say the least. But Oliver was a human, and Heracles was a demigod. He couldn't even compete.

"Are you ready?" Oliver asked, his voice shaky.

I nodded.

"Don't give up, Elyse," Heracles repeated.

I turned to him.

"I'm going out now. Like a normal girl." I forced a smile on my face, but all I managed was a lopsided grin.

"Come back when you're done," he said.

I shrugged one shoulder. "We'll see."

When Oliver and I left my apartment, Oliver glanced over his shoulder.

"Is he going to let himself out?"

"Yeah," I said.

"He seems…nice."

I nodded. "You know what it's like with family. Always some drama."

Oliver chuckled nervously. "I guess I should be happy he's your cousin."

I nodded without really hearing what Oliver was saying. My mind mulled over Heracles's words, even though I'd been determined to discard them completely. I couldn't do this anymore. I wasn't cut out for this life. I was alone, isolated—without anyone to understand what I went through. And now I was heartbroken too. This was bullshit.

If I moved with the humans, living the life they led, I could have trivial problems and friends to turn to about problems. I would never feel like I didn't fit in, except... Dad... I couldn't abandon the cause.

Yes, my family would be disappointed in me.

But who the fuck cared? They were dead.

Oliver drove us to the small restaurant that looked small and romantic. We parked in the street. He opened the car door for me like a gentleman and offered me his arm when we strolled the short distance to the restaurant. Clouds formed above us, and thunder and lightning warred across the sky.

"Looks like rain," Oliver said, looking up.

I nodded, not wanting to give the weather any thought, considering how much of it was impacted by the gods.

We arrived at the door when a terrible wind picked up, whipping my long hair around my face.

"Let's get you inside." Oliver's arm sailed around my waist to supposedly protect me from the storm when another clap of thunder crackled all around us and lightning lit up the sky. In the bright light, a silhouette appeared to be descending. My stomach hardened to cement. What now?

"Elyse," a deep voice boomed, and I twisted my head.

A sturdy man marched toward me, arms swinging by his side, dressed in a toga. He wore power and confidence, the flowing white fabric draped over a shoulder and around his muscular body, his manly chest on display. He had a long, bushy beard with piercing blue eyes like the sky and a strong nose and chin, reminding me of Heracles. But he wasn't old and could easily be mistaken for Heracles's brother. A lightning bolt struck overhead.

Oh, fuck! Zeus! The ruler of Olympian gods was on Earth. My feet froze in place, my mouth gaping open. Was it really him coming toward me?

Of course, he would look like nothing more than a human to Oliver, but he would still be huge. The gods didn't like taking the form of the weak and weary, even though that would have been a better disguise.

"Do you know this guy?" Oliver asked when Zeus approached us. He sounded worried. If only he knew the truth.

"I'm her uncle," Zeus declared as if he'd heard what Heracles had said to me. Probably had, and in his company, I found myself trembling. Warmth fluttered through me, an energy that raised the hairs on my arms, yet soothed me. Just as my dad had made me feel after we'd lost my mom and brothers. He reminded me I wasn't alone and those I lost would always be with me in spirit. So was this Zeus's energy affecting me? A fatherly figure, looking out for me? I must have been mistaken, and yet I couldn't ignore the comfort settling in my chest in his company.

"You have a lot of family around," Oliver said, eyeing Zeus, unsure where to put his hands.

"Apparently," I said, then turned to Zeus. "What do you want?" I didn't sound very friendly, but I wasn't in the mood lately for niceties, considering his so-called blessing had landed me in this situation.

"We need to talk," he growled.

I started shaking my head, but then I changed my mind, especially when everything about him reminded me about

169

my dad. Okay, not physically, but the tenderness in his eyes, how close he stood, as if he'd protect me from the world if he had to, and even the way he tilted his head slightly to the right when he studied me. But this was Zeus, not my father, and I actually had a hell of a lot to say to the king of Olympian gods.

"I'll meet you inside," I said to Oliver.

He looked reluctant at first, but Zeus pinned him with a stare that could melt his face, and I nodded encouragingly. Oliver's expression softened and he disappeared into the restaurant.

Zeus snorted. "You're wasting your time with the mortals."

"I'm one of them, remember?" I said, stepping back down to the sidewalk. Maybe I should have been more respectful. There were gods for every small thing, but there was a kind of hierarchy among them all, and Zeus was on top. But I was in a shitty mood. I couldn't exactly wake up from the dead and be full of smiles and unicorns.

"This fight isn't over," Zeus insisted, his voice lowering as if trying to appeal to my reasonable side.

"Yes, it is," I replied. "I'm not doing this. The power you gave me is great and all, but I don't want it anymore. You can take it. Bless someone else."

Zeus shook his head, his white hair bouncing over his shoulders. His eyes were as bright as Heracles's, and he had the same bronze tan as his son.

"You can't give up," Zeus repeated, as if not listening to my decision.

"Really?" I asked, fire spinning through me. I sported a broken heart, and he wanted me to just pretend none of that affected me. But fuck it. Apollo watching me die tore me to shreds. I didn't mean anywhere near as much to him as I'd thought I did. "Watch me."

170

"Who will look after them when you don't?"

"Who will look after me if I do?" I asked, sucking in sharp breaths. I didn't want this life any longer. It was filled with pain, and I wasn't talking about being stabbed to death. It was about who had stabbed me. About Hades and Apollo. I didn't want to play this game anymore.

Yet in my mind all I could remember was a similar argument I'd had with Dad when I'd wanted friends and boyfriends to hang out with. And it always came back to responsibility, the blessing on our family. Just like now.

"You're interrupting my date," I said, lifting my chin before turning around and walking away, but the heavens opened, and rain poured down in sheets so suddenly, it drenched me completely. My makeup would be smudged.

I spun around. "I've had enough of this shit!" I shouted, and I reached down deep, finding the strength that had been building in my core. Instinct controlled me, the rage burning at my core at the thought that I'd been betrayed, the sorrow of being tricked into believing Apollo had wanted me. Without a thought, I grabbed the power with both hands and threw it at Zeus with all the strength I could muster.

Just as I had done to my father... except I had thrown a textbook at him, hitting him right in the head and giving him the biggest bruise.

Zeus staggered backward, his eyes widening as if shocked by my attack. My head screamed at me to stop being a fool, but heartbreak did awful things to people. Right now, the power surged, rising through me like electricity, dancing on my skin. I could taste the magic, smell the burnt scene, feel it light up my body as if I were a conductor.

This was new. I stared down the sparks skipping over my arms, shaking from the uncertainty because I was sick and tired of surprises.

"What's happening?" I asked.

When I glanced up at Zeus, his eyes were made of light, his hands glowing. The heavens thundered, and a brilliant shock of white played across the skies, touching down all around us. He was pissed off, and he had reason to be. I was a human, his creation for all intents and purposes, and I had poked the bear.

"Stop!" Heracles shouted, jumping in between the two of us right as Zeus threw a bolt at me. Heracles caught it, and only fractures of the blaze reached me. It burned me, leaving red marks on my skin that looked like the lightning that played across the sky.

"Father, stop!" Heracles shouted. "She doesn't know."

"Know what?" I demanded, staring at the two power-houses glaring at each other. Heracles reached his father in height, both strong and muscular and teeming energy, their skin beaming with sparks.

"Then, teach her," Zeus growled in a voice that sounded like the thunder itself. "Because next time, I won't stop."

Heracles nodded and turned to me, his eyes soft.

"Just calm down," he said in low tones. "Keep it under control until he leaves."

The power played over my skin the moment I thought about the energy, its strength threatened to snap out of control. It was leaking away like sand—the tighter I held on to it, the more ran through my fingers, getting away from me. The tingles underneath my skin heightened as if someone had attached a live wire to my nerves.

"I can't control it!" I cried out, my knees weakening.

"Just breathe. Find your center. Think about something other than your power, something that calms you."

My mind jumped from one thing to the next. I sifted through memories, trying to find something to anchor myself to. My parents, my brothers, the family dinners around the large table in the kitchen. Artisan coffee with

Catina, black-and-white photos of beautiful people, the training sessions with Heracles when we ran for miles. Nothing worked. I sped through, looking for something, anything that would do the trick.

When I finally found something, it was the way Apollo had looked at me when he had been on top of me in my bed. His large body covered mine, pinning me down and filling me up. His hair hung around his face, and his eyes were piercing blue like nothing the sky had been lately. Warmth beat down on my skin as if I were lying in the sun.

The power receded back into me, and I could breathe easy again, knowing it wasn't going to get away from me. I focused on the image of Apollo's face, drinking in the heat that came from him, drowning in the pain that accompanied it after he'd ditched me.

I wouldn't focus on that now, though. I needed to stay in control, not let it take me over again.

When Heracles touched my arm, I jumped and nearly dropped the hold on my power, letting it loose again.

"He's gone," Heracles explained.

It had stopped raining, and steel gray clouds faded away into a monochromatic landscape. Heracles was as drenched as I was, his hair clinging to his face, his white shirt see-through to show off his god body.

"Come on. Let's get you home," Heracles said. "We have a lot to talk about."

"What exactly just happened?' I asked, my head still spinning, especially from seeing Zeus. He'd personally come to ensure I didn't give up on the cause, which in hindsight was massive. But I was too consumed by anger and the energy rattling through me to make proper sense of everything.

"Every time you die, you come back stronger. It's a trade or something. I've never seen energy like this, though. We have work to do for you to control it."

I stared over my shoulder to the restaurant, remembering Oliver. "He's waiting for me."

"I suggest you tell him you can't do the date tonight. We need to get this under control before you hurt someone—or yourself. If you lose it over dinner, it's going to get ugly with all those humans."

I nodded, hating the notion that anyone had to fear me, feeling guilty for letting Oliver down. He'd always been kind to me and here I was about to ditch him. But Heracles was right. I should have known I could never have a normal life. I wasn't cut out to be a regular girl. It sucked, but a regular woman would never be able to do what I had been put on Earth for.

Only I could do that.

CHAPTER 21

Apollo

*A*fter Hades killed Elyse, the darkness started to withdraw. X's power subsided, the monster fading away enough for the lights of the city to penetrate the night again.

Hades looked as ragged as I felt. But all I could think about was her death. I experienced every ache and pain she had to her last dying breath. I had sensed her life exiting her body, tearing away from me, leaving me behind alone. It was like the sun had disappeared, and there was only the cold to keep me company.

"You look like shit," Hades snarled.

"I tried." My voice came out softer than I'd intended. "I tried to stop Death, but he's not going to back down. He's drawing his strength from the souls he devours. He's growing more potent with every kill."

Hades nodded and sighed. His eyes were lifeless, his voice dull. "The souls don't come to me. Their lifeforce feeds him.

And I can't stop him, either, but he's breaking the natural flow of the universe."

Hades looked at Elyse's dead body on the sidewalk. She was limp on the ground in a puddle of blood that had finally stopped flowing. A bubble had formed around her, a supernatural shield that kept her body safe while she wasn't in it, and no mortal could get to her to do any harm.

"I had to do it." Hades sounded like death himself. His voice cracked at the end, and his face grew pale. The Greek god looked like he had died, his eyes dull, his posture defeated.

"I know," I said, but my words were barren of comfort when the agony still burrowed through me.

"She would never have stopped hunting X, but she wasn't strong enough and whether it was today or in a week's time when she confronted him, he would've killed her for good. And she wouldn't come back from that." He paused, staring at his blood-stained hands. "She'd never listen to us or change her mind, so I did something to make her more powerful. To save her," he murmured.

We stood together in silence for a while before Hades turned to me. His expression was filled with raw emotion, vulnerability, agony. I was one of the few who would see him like this. He cared for her. I had seen it when he'd confronted me outside her apartment. And I saw it now. Killing her had destroyed him too.

"Take care of her," Hades instructed, his expression downcast, his voice already distant. "Make sure she gets home safe."

"Don't you want to come with me?" I asked.

Hades shook his head, his hands pressed into his pockets. "Not after what I did. I can never forget that and she will never forgive me."

He walked away from me, his posture curled forward, his

chin tucked into his chest. A cloud formed around him like black smoke, and after a few steps, it was as if the darkness had swallowed him whole.

I turned and approached Elyse. Her eyes were still open, staring lifelessly at me. Guilt threatened to choke me. I made the right decision, but it had been the worst thing I'd ever had to do.

Almost as horrible as what Hades had to live through right now.

I reached down for her, the magical shield sizzling along my arm, and closed Elyse's eyes with my fingers, careful not to hurt her in any way. When I lifted her up, her body was limp and weighed nothing at all. Her head lolled to the side when I raised her in my arms, and I tucked her against my chest. My throat choked at seeing her this way, and all I could picture was the moment the life had left her gorgeous eyes.

I staggered back to her apartment, cradling her, whispering poetry as if she could hear me. Humans couldn't see me carrying her lifeless body as I concealed us, and it felt like I was left alone in this world. Her place was far, but she deserved to be treated with respect. I wasn't going to throw her on the back of my bike.

When I reached her apartment, I carried her through the walls with magic and to the bedroom, then laid her on the bed. I left her bloody clothes on her body, made sure she wasn't lying on her braid, and stepped back.

I hoped Zeus would stick to his word and bring her back. I couldn't lose her. Not like this. Not after Hades had taken her. Not after I'd stood against her.

Watching over her the whole night, I sat there, staring at her, willing her to wake up, which I knew wouldn't happen. It would take days. Yet I didn't move from her side, each second dragging, the incident whirring through my mind on repeat, over and over. Reminding me of what I'd done. Of course, it was for her safety, but it didn't stop the emptiness flooding me. When I finally decided to leave, I felt hollow inside, but watching her killed me.

The weekend came and went in a drunken blur that was laced with whiskey and tequila and vodka. I drank until I couldn't stand anymore. I passed out in my bed and woke up again the next morning, ready for the next round. There were upsides and downsides to being a god. It took fucking forever to get drunk, but the bounce back rate was spectacular.

By Monday, I was a wreck. The alcohol hadn't helped at all.

I had felt it when she'd come back to life. It was like a jolt of electricity sent through my own heart like someone was resuscitating me. My pulse pounded through my veins, and I shot to my feet, shaking all over.

I couldn't get her face out of my mind. Her eyes, pleading for me to save her. Then, the realization that I wouldn't. She had been devastated. I had killed her before Hades did.

Elyse had always been a fighter. It was what had drawn me to her in the first place. Elyse was different than any of the women I had met before. Human and divine. I'd longed to keep her by my side.

It was better this way. If I wasn't with her, Zeus wouldn't kick me back to Mount Olympus, and my life could carry on as usual.

Except after being with Elyse, life as I had known it was over.

Being drunk didn't exactly help, either. It numbed the feelings, but it didn't stop me from thinking. Or remembering.

I couldn't take it anymore. It was driving me crazy. Zeus was going to fuck me up if he found out what I was going to do, but I refused to keep drinking myself into a stupor to forget if it did nothing to drive the images of her away.

I left the bar I had chosen to grace with my presence and took a cab to her apartment building. She wasn't there. But her scent was all over the place and the apartment hummed with her energy. Just being in her living space charged me as if I had been plugged in after running on reserves for days.

With closed eyes, I drove my powers out to the corners of the Earth, searching for her, longing to connect with her. I had been with Elyse. We had orgasmed together. The connection that had been forged as a result had linked me to her so I could find her anywhere.

She was close. Her scent drifted on the breeze. Her warmth radiated all around me.

I followed the feeling, and she was surprisingly far, considering how strong the signal had been when I'd reached out for her. When I finally tracked her down, she was strolling out of an office building.

"Elyse," I called out.

She looked up at me, and the life drained out of her eyes. Her lips pursed into a thin line, turning them almost white. But she was beautiful and healthy and strong, and by Zeus, her power was like electricity all around her, even when she stood a few feet away.

"I have nothing to say to you," she said tightly as she marched toward a nearby L train station.

"Then I'll do the talking," I insisted.

"I don't want to hear it." She spoke with her back to me.

I jogged after her as she headed down the sidewalk. When I reached her, she spun around and put her hands on my chest. She had wanted to push me away, I was sure of it. But the moment we'd touched, we were shaken. Our connection was so strong, it left us both breathless.

"Did you feel that?" Elyse asked in a labored voice.

I nodded. Her power was intense, burning in my veins, luring me closer. The sexual tension escalated between us. I could take her right now, and I knew it would be even more spectacular than it had been the first time.

But this wasn't about sex—it was about something so much deeper. I had to talk to her. Only talk.

"You deserted me," Elyse blurted out, her eyes glistening. "You were supposed to be my hero, and you let him kill me."

"X was coming for you," I explained, my arms hanging stiffly by my side. "If he'd gotten to you before Hades had, you wouldn't have woken up again."

She looked at me with a face that was riddled with questions.

"I would rather you died and came back to life than died and I lost you forever," I added.

Elyse shook her head. "I needed you." Her voice croaked, and my hands tingled with the urge to take her into my arms, show her she meant the world to me, make her see we'd saved her.

"I know," I said instead. "It's killing me. I'm so sorry."

Elyse shook her head again. She looked at my chest, not my eyes. I couldn't tell what was running through her mind. "If you helped me instead of going into the darkness..."

"You would have died in my arms, and I wouldn't have been able to get you back. I can't stand the thought of losing you, Elyse. Can't you see? This was the only way."

A tear rolled down her cheek. "I guess I kind of understand," she finally said.

But did she really? I lifted my hand and brushed the tear from her face.

"I tried to stay away from you," I said. "Since the moment I first saw you, I've been drawn to you, and I can't stay away. Being with you can only cause trouble, but for all my god powers, I can't fight what I feel for you."

"And what's that?" Elyse asked, her voice brave once again. She looked up at me, her dark eyes deep, her face open, her heart pure.

"I've fallen for you. It might ruin me, but I'm in love with you." I placed my hand on Elyse's cheek, and she turned her face into my palm, placing her hand over mine. Her fingers were long and thin, the touch of her skin like the first rays of dawn.

"I think I've fallen for you too," Elyse admitted in a whisper. "That's why what you did hurts so damn much."

I put a bent finger under her chin and tipped her face up to me. I brushed my lips against hers, and the moment we kissed, my energy flared up and hers rose to meet it. It wasn't so strange anymore, having a godly connection with a human, but I would never get used to the feel of her energy rubbing up against mine, brushing against my body like fur, licking my skin with heat that I could bathe in.

I ran my hands down Elyse's back and onto her ass, squeezing it. She pressed her body up against mine, and my dick responded, taking its cue to stand at attention. The sexual tension came thick and fast, and I wanted to drag Elyse away to a quiet place and make her mine, proving to her what she meant to me. I wanted to promise myself to her for eternity.

But she broke the kiss. The power drew sticky strings between us when she stepped away.

"I can't do this right now," she whispered, as if struggling to voice the words. "I have a life to get back on track. I nearly lost a big contract in the human world because of all this. And X is still out there. My job is to help humans, and you will always stand in my way."

She stood on her tiptoes and pressed her lips against mine again. I melted a little.

"I'll see you soon, okay?"

I nodded, dazed. Lost. Confused. Broken.

When Elyse stepped backward and turned away, her words sunk in, so I grabbed her wrist.

"Promise me you won't go after X alone," I demanded.

Elyse hesitated. "Someone has to stop him."

"Just wait until we figure something out. I'll do everything I can."

She finally nodded.

"I won't do anything stupid," she said. I released her wrist, and she rushed toward the L train station. It was only after she vanished around a corner that I realized she hadn't promised me anything at all.

CHAPTER 22

Elyse

*A*fter Apollo had left me to die at Hades's hand, I had been bursting with fury at him, convinced the son of a bitch had betrayed me. Then he'd found me and explained what had happened. The whole thing spun in my head because I understood why he hadn't helped me battle Hades. I got it, but the memory sat so fresh in my mind, I kept having to remind myself Apollo had my best interest at heart. And that sonofabitch X had used his influence over me to drive me insane with rage. To fight without thinking through the consequences. He'd wanted to battle me so he could finish me.

But I trusted Apollo. I had seen what he'd looked like when he'd stepped out of the darkness that night. As if something had been draining his life force. As a god, he had an infinite amount of energy, but X was getting stronger.

Apollo had saved me, just not in the way I had asked him to.

And he loved me.

I was floating on sunshine.

When I thought about his words, warmth spread through my body. It was the heat that came with Apollo, the fire that had started to define him for me. That wasn't the only heat that came with him. When I was with him, I couldn't deny the sexual need that built between us, the urge to be together, completely connected.

I had wanted to be with him so badly when he had cornered me, and I would have loved nothing more than to take him back to my place and let him apologize to me with his body again and again.

But I had to get my head straight first, not drown in our mingled powers. Concentrate on how I'd deal with X and be smart. Not rush things. And maybe all wasn't lost for us yet.

I had a portfolio to send to a potential client, and photos to edit for *Foundation*, where I had managed, by some miracle, not to lose the contract after missing the meeting. The perfect distraction. I always found it easy to work through solutions as I edited my photos.

X was still out there, sucking the life force out of humans, draining them of their power for personal gain. The more people X killed, the more potent he grew.

There was no doubt—I had to stop X before he became unstoppable, and then no one could stand in his way.

I was stronger now. I had learned from Heracles that with every death, my strength increased upon coming back. Too bad I could only die so many times before it was final, and if X consumed too many souls, I wouldn't be able to stand up to him no matter what.

Something had to be done before that happened.

Apollo didn't want me to fight X alone. I understood it, but I had a duty to the people on Earth, imparted by Zeus himself. I was going to make sure we got through this with as few casualties as possible. We had already lost too many.

When I arrived at my apartment, I sent the portfolio off and uploaded the photos to my laptop, but my concertation was all over the place. Screw the work, I had to find a way to stop X. I dressed in workout clothes, undid my hair, and braided it again so it was tighter than before, and headed out to meet Heracles.

He'd been training me to harness my new power. I'd been fighting with different weapons while we waited for my replacements to arrive on special order. And I was ready to learn more.

"How are you feeling today?" Heracles asked with a smile when he reached the training center.

"Great," I said, that earlier joy still teeming through me.

Heracles nodded, but he looked suspicious, his eyes narrowing in my direction. "You look like you're glowing. What happened?"

I shrugged. I wasn't going to tell him about my run-in with Apollo. Not yet. Maybe not ever. He would figure it out sooner or later, I was sure.

We headed out of the parking lot and down the street on our run.

"What are we going to do about X?" I asked.

"What do you mean 'we'?" Heracles cut me a sharp look.

Our feet beat a tattoo on the tarmac. My legs were a lot shorter than Heracles's, and I had to run a lot faster to keep up with him. I needed the exercise anyway, and Heracles had never taken it easy on me.

"He's still out there, devouring souls," I insisted. "He has to be stopped."

"Yeah, I know. But this is not my fight," Heracles grumbled.

I stopped running. Heracles took a few more steps before he realized I wasn't next to him, and he slowed and turned.

"What?" I demanded.

"You heard me," he said. He wasn't even breathing hard. I was heaving and sweating already. Heracles had been pushing the pace a little more than usual.

"I died," I said. "What if it happens again?"

"Then you come back to life again."

I shook my head. "You know that's not going to keep happening, right?"

Heracles put his hands on his hips and looked up at the heavens. I wondered if he could see Mount Olympus when he did that, or if he was conferring with Zeus or something.

"I had my appointment with death long ago," he said after a bit. "When I died as a human and was transformed into an immortal by Zeus. I'm not going there again."

I couldn't believe it, and I pinched the bridge of my nose. "People are dying. Every day."

"I'm only a mentor, Elyse. I'm not their hero. You are." His voice remained calm, as if he'd practiced having this argument with me.

"I can't do it alone," I huffed and started running again.

"So get allies." He joined me, jogging with me.

"Like who?"

Heracles thought about it for a moment, staring ahead at the oversized fountain we passed in Grant Park.

"I'll ask Zeus to send you help," he finally said.

"All my allies are dead, or they've abandoned the cause so long ago, they don't know what they are anymore," I said. "Who can help me?"

"I don't know. But I'll ask," Heracles said. "Leave it with me."

"What makes you think Zeus will send someone?"

Heracles shrugged. His enormous shoulders moved up and down and the muscles rippled under the skin when he did. "We'll see what he has in mind. When he gave you your power, it was to save the humans from the creatures that X

186

sent to Earth to slaughter them. But X himself hadn't been a problem in the past. Something went wrong for X to be here now."

I thought about Hades and how his presence coincided with X arriving. For a while I had assumed X had had nothing to do with Hades, but that had been before the god had killed me. Now every time I pictured Hades, my stomach churned with uncertainty, reminding me that I wasn't sure of his real intentions and he had his own agenda.

"Zeus didn't choose a person," Heracles continued. "He chose a family. Strength in numbers and all that, as you've said before. I'll ask."

I nodded. There wasn't much else I could say to that.

We ran through the park for the next hour before we finally circled around to the training center again. We drank water from our bottles in front of the doors, the light breeze cooling me down. The sky was clearer today. Clouds were still littered across it, but the sun broke through in patches.

"The weather is wonderful today," I said. "It's nice to have a bit of sun."

"Looks like Apollo is in a good mood," Heracles responded.

I frowned. Apollo was the god of the sun too. I had never considered that the miserable weather and the absence of sun in Chicago had been him.

"Come on," Heracles said, strolling inside the building when his water was finished. "We have training to do."

And I was ready, so I followed him.

After several hours of knife throwing, jujitsu, kickboxing and fencing, I was tired and sweaty and drained. My muscles ached, but in that good way that filled me with determination. Practicing with my new energy was fun—as if I had unlocked a new level—but I had to concentrate the whole time to keep myself in check and not lose control. I had worked for so long pushing to release my power that now I couldn't reel it in if I didn't concentrate. Too much strength was as dangerous as not enough of the stuff against the gods, and I hadn't found the middle ground yet.

It was emotionally consuming to keep myself in check. I had to channel my energy in a different way than before, and that would mean lots of exercise.

I showered, grabbed something to eat, and sat down in front of my laptop to start editing the photos for *Foundation*. The sooner I finished the project, the better. The boss there had been gracious enough to give me a second chance, but it was only thanks to Catina that I still had the contract in the first place. I had been so distracted by fighting the gods and taking care of the mythical business I had been born into that I'd neglected my human life. My portfolio and my name as a freelance photographer depended on *Foundation* in a big way.

It took me a while to get into the swing of concentrating on the job, to focus my attention on the photos, and do what needed to be done. I had finally caught up in my work, the radio blaring in the background to drown out the sounds of the city around me, when I became aware of a faint knocking sound.

When I turned off the radio, the sound was clearer.

I hurried to the door and opened it. Oliver stood in front of me. Shit, I hadn't even spoken to him since the night of our date. Fire crawled up my cheeks. He was probably here to give me a mouthful.

"Can I come in?" he asked, his voice serious, no trace of his usually nervous self. I was hesitant, but I nodded. I owed him this much.

"Want anything to drink?" I asked politely. The air between us felt strained as if the walls were closing in around me as I felt a deep conversation was coming my way.

"No, thank you," Oliver said.

"Okay. Come sit down." We sat down opposite each other on the couches, and I dropped my gaze, waiting for him to speak.

"Do you want to go out with me again?" Oliver asked, straight to the point.

I looked down at my nails. They were always short and sensible. Long nails could scratch, but they could also break in a fight and that hurt like a bitch.

"I don't think that's a good idea, Oliver," I responded gently. "I'm sorry."

He shook his head. "I don't understand. We didn't even have dinner before you ran out on me."

"I know. I'm sorry about that, but our paths don't align."

"How do you know?" Oliver's brow pinched. "You don't even know me."

I nodded. "You're right. I don't. But I'm always going to be running out on you for one reason or another. My life doesn't have space in it for anyone right now."

"Or maybe it just doesn't have room for me," Oliver said bitterly. "I've seen the type of men who come and go here. Steroid junkies. I know I can never look like that, but I have good qualities."

I couldn't help but smile. That was how they looked to him?

"I'm sorry, Oliver," I insisted. "I wish we could have worked somehow. I wish there was something to pursue, but we don't fit."

The truth was, I had accepted who I was. For the time being anyway. I'd realized that I would never fit into the mediocrity that would come with pretending to be human. I would never be able to live a mundane life, purely for the sake of getting through each day. And especially when my heart fluttered each time I thought of Apollo.

I hadn't been born for that, and if I abandoned what I had

been born to do, I wouldn't only be letting my family down, taking away everything they had sacrificed themselves for, but I would be letting myself down.

And that was not acceptable.

"There's no reason why we can't be friends," I said to Oliver.

He smiled bitterly. "Yeah. Friend. That's what men want when they look at you." He sighed and shook his head. "I guess it was worth a shot."

"I'm flattered, Oliver. Really."

He nodded without saying anything and stood. "I'm still next door if you need a cup of sugar," he said.

"Thanks," I said, walking him to the door. When he stepped out, he turned and looked like he wanted to say something, but he changed his mind.

"Just be careful of the company you keep," he warned.

"I will," I said, then closed the door. Poor Oliver. Be careful of the company I keep? He had no idea.

CHAPTER 23

Hades

Fuck this place. Earth was a horrible place. I had thought the Underworld was dull and drab, but there was so much fucking pain on Earth, I didn't know how the humans could stand it.

I had been in a shitty mood since the night when Elyse wouldn't back the fuck down, and I'd had to go to the extreme to stop her from getting herself killed by X.

Except, I'd killed her instead. What did that make me? I had wanted to be a hero. But I had been the person she'd fought. I had been the one to rip her away from this world, to stab her into oblivion so she would come back less one life.

I felt like an asshole for doing this to someone who had touched me so deeply.

I hadn't been able to do anything else, though. The bitch could fight. I had to hand it to her. If I hadn't finished her, I would have had to watch her die. She would have gotten past me and run to X, looking her death in the face and smelling the rot on his breath. Even knocking her out wouldn't have worked because she'd be up in no time, healing quicker than your average human, and take on X again. I knew if she died, she'd be out for days and be reborn with stronger powers. I was under no illusion she would stop hunting down X, but now she had stronger abilities.

Apollo had been there, and it was only because of him that Elyse was alive and kicking now. Albeit less one life. Apollo had gone into that darkness, holding back X for as long as he could.

Gods couldn't die, but he had been damn close. X had tried to consume him too. It had been the only reason X hadn't reached Elyse. I had been able to hold her back, but I was only one god, and I hadn't been able to restrain X, either.

I wished I knew what X was doing here. The mother-fucker had come to Earth when I had, and he claimed he had no clue what his goal was, but it scared the shit out of even me. And I lived around death, so that was saying something. I didn't know how he had come here, but everyone seemed to blame me.

No one deserved to die before their time. X was fucking with the careful balance the Fates held in their hands, and that wasn't okay.

Something was wrong, and I didn't know what it was or how to make it right.

I was on a mission to cause destruction. I didn't kill the way everyone thought I did. Hades was not the god of Death, contrary to popular belief. I left the humans alone, but I wasn't a nice guy, and I was pissed off at myself, furious that I'd killed Elyse, enraged that X was loose, angry at everything. I'd been pacing in my home, unable to stand still, my mind on constant edge, my muscles tense.

My pitchfork was my weapon of choice. Even though it had been used to take one of Elyse's lives, I wasn't going to get rid of it because the pitchfork was like an extension of me.

Instead, I used it to break shit. I broke bus stops. Dragged it along the road so there were holes and ditches, then touched patches of grass in the park, the lawn shriveling up and dying. I couldn't see anything beautiful without thinking of Elyse.

So I destroyed everything in my way.

"Hey!" someone shouted, and her voice sliced through me like a knife. She was furious, but it was a voice that would always tug at my heart. "You're destroying public property."

I smiled, and it wasn't a pretty grin. When I turned around to face her, a jolt of electricity shot through me. Elyse looked as amazing as ever, her body every bit a warrior. It was as if she had become even more so. Her hair was thick and glossy, and her eyes bright. I had watched her die, but the woman who stood before me was perfect. She wore her usual leather pants, yet her top was sleeveless, and she wore leather sheaths on her arms. Her hair was pulled back in a braid, but something about her was sexy in a deadly way.

Snap out of it, I told myself. I couldn't afford to care for her. Killing her when I had feelings for her had nearly destroyed me too.

"What are you going to do about it?" I taunted. It was safer than being nice.

Elyse pulled two long, thin knives from her wrist sheaths.

"I've got some new toys I've been dying to try out," she said, and she swung them around and around at her sides, her hips swinging from side to side as she came to me.

Fuck me, she was hot as hell.

Elyse broke into a run, and she came toward me, knives low at her thighs, her speed impressive.

When she reached me, I was ready for her, but this was going to be a challenge.

"You've become stronger," I said as I blocked one of her knives with my pitchfork and spun out of reach of the other.

"You're awake for a change," Elyse quipped.

"If this is what I get when I kill you, maybe I should do it more often."

It was a low blow. I knew that. Elyse's face darkened. "Bring it on, asshole."

The word stung a little. It shouldn't have. I had told myself I would stop caring.

Elyse and I fought across the road, moving back and forth as she pushed toward me and then she had to back away as I counterattacked. But this was more than a fight, more of a dance of our powers, the unspoken words hanging over us that neither of us wanted to say. That despite the fucked-up hell between us, I could never hate her. And I saw the same in her eyes.

We ended up in an enormous green park. I wasn't sure which one.

Elyse sliced my arm with her knife, and I hissed, darkness seeping out of my skin. She had every right to be pissed off at me, but I had saved her life, goddammit. Couldn't she see that? Maybe I'd mistaken the look in her eyes for longing, when in fact, it was revenge she yearned for.

I willed a snake into being. Reptiles were my animals, and I could bring them to life whenever I wanted them. The creature tangled around Elyse's leg, and she tripped and fell to the ground. It wasn't poisonous. I had no intention of killing her again. I just wanted to have it out with her. I wanted to take the edge off. Usually, sex worked for me. But as much as I wanted it, that wasn't going to happen with Elyse today.

Or anytime soon. So I'd take a battle.

"You guys are entertaining as fuck," a male said when I pinned Elyse to the ground with my pitchfork. She had dropped her knives to grasp onto the pitchfork, stopping it from breaking skin.

We both froze and turned our heads. The humans couldn't see us fight. We hadn't ever had an audience, so it couldn't be anyone mortal being entertained by us.

Ares leaned against a tree, his dark skin glowing as if he had recently been oiled. He wore leather armor complete with his boots, and his sword hung at his side. He wasn't wearing his helmet for once.

"Who are you?" Elyse demanded, using my distraction against me and throwing me off balance, getting out from underneath the pitchfork.

"Ares, at your service. I believe you needed a sidekick." He stood there cocky as hell.

Elyse and I both gaped at Ares.

"You're not wanted here, dickhead," I growled.

Ares laughed, the sound sharp and loud. All for show, of course. "It never changes, does it?"

"It's your shitty haircut that does it," I said.

Ares's dark hair was buzzed down to his scalp. His face was square and mischievous.

He laughed again. "After centuries, I thought you would have come up with a new line."

Elyse shook her head. "Why are you here again?" So she didn't know what the son of a bitch was doing here, either.

"Zeus sent me. You asked for help to fight this war. I'm here to help." He winked her way, as if he were the hero swooping in to save the day. Not in my lifetime—or any for that matter.

I chuckled, louder. "What a fucking joke. You? Here to help? You know this is serious, right?"

Ares didn't look amused, shadows gliding under his narrowing eyes, his lips thinning. "I am the god of war." His words boomed, echoing around us.

"More like god of *his own agenda*." I laughed at my own joke.

Ares's shoulders curled forward, tossing daggers with his gaze. I wanted him that way. But if he was here to help Elyse, he could fuck off. The only way to get him to do exactly what he wasn't supposed to was to get him riled up. Ares was full of shit on a good day. He was supposed to be the god of war, but he was a coward when it came down to standing up for what he believed in, and he was a loose cannon in every other regard. The piece of shit would only make matters worse, not better.

The sooner Elyse realized she couldn't depend on this asswipe, the better.

"You know what? Fuck you, too, Hades," Ares said, flipping me off.

"You sound like you're in high school," I said.

"You're taunting him." Elyse raised a brow, glaring my way.

I shrugged. "So? He's not here for me. He's here for you. I owe him nothing."

Ares pushed off the tree he leaned against, his shoulders squaring. It was exactly what I'd wanted. He shot up into the air. Ares could fly, all right.

Elyse mustn't have known about his skill, for she watched him with shock and amazement. It would have been cute if I hadn't been so busy watching where Ares was going to come down.

His sword was pointed down at me when he descended toward me, and I lifted my pitchfork. When Elyse and I fought, she was a worthy opponent. But Ares? He was wasting my time.

When our weapons hit each other, a shockwave of magic circled out from us, flattening everything in our immediate surroundings—the nearby trees had fallen over, the shrubs squashed. The energy rippled out to make the rest of the city tremble. Elyse was on her back, gasping. Car alarms were going off, and trash cans and bus stops were dented. The benches that had been placed at intervals were broken or shattered.

"What the fuck?" Elyse shouted, sitting up. "Ares, what are you doing?"

"Fighting this asshole."

"You're supposed to help me, not make it worse," she snarled. Ares pulled up his shoulders and looked around. I was willing to hold off on another attack and watch this.

"Are you planning on fixing this?" Elyse asked him. She was sexy when she got angry.

"Sorry," Ares said with an attitude that suggested he wasn't sorry at all.

"I'll leave you two to it then," I said, strolling away.

Elyse let out a cry of frustration. I smirked as I left them. She wanted to have it out with me, get her fury out, but knowing Ares was shitting on her parade was great. I didn't have to do anything now.

Because the truth was I didn't want to battle her. Such engagements with her made me hard for her. I couldn't help it. But I didn't want to fight her. I wanted to fuck her. It wasn't about her body, either. I fantasized about being with her and I hadn't felt like this about anyone since Persephone way in the beginning. But that hadn't been real in the end.

I understood Elyse still hated me, and that sucked balls, but I had to accept the situation because how could I ever take back killing her? I had done it for the right reasons. But it stung like a bitch.

It was better if I stayed away from her. She would only distract me, and I had left the Underworld to get away from women who distracted me. Not that Elyse was like Persephone, but I refused to have my heart broken again.

Still, I craved Elyse so badly, my whole body ache, but I had to be realistic. She was a mortal and represented trouble. It felt like the more she hung around me, the more things went wrong. I had a feeling I was the problem, and the last thing I needed was to be the reason something happened to her, something I wouldn't be able to prevent next time.

Except things had gone terribly wrong.

I'd killed her, my hand forced because my emotions had driven me. I adored her and had understood the decision would result in me losing her. And it had fucking devastated me to drive that pitchfork into her heart. To eliminate her life. The image hadn't left my mind. Neither had the pleading in her eyes, the fear of losing her grip, well aware of what was coming her way. And I'd been the one to deliver the blow that would stay with me for eternity.

Son of a bitch, I was the god of the Underworld, yet I pined after a mortal who had crawled into my heart. No denying the truth hammering into me.

I'd lost her. So I'd walk away. Admit my loss.

I would stay away from her rather than get involved. Because if I started to get involved in any way, I was fucked.

CHAPTER 24

Elyse

"*Y*ou're just walking away from me?" I called out. "We were in the middle of something."

Maybe it looked pathetic that I was running after Hades, but I was pissed off at him, and I hadn't gotten it out of my system yet. I hated that he was so disinterested.

"Looks like you have your hands full, sweetheart," Hades said with a smirk.

"Don't call me that," I snapped.

"I'm going," Hades said. "I'm not in the mood for his shit." He gestured with his head toward Ares. He looked bored, but it was a façade because this was Hades. The guy didn't just stroll away from a fight. He was hiding something from me. I couldn't see it as much as I could feel it.

I took a step forward, closing the distance between us. "You can't leave."

"And why is that?" He cut me a sarcastic look, as if he knew exactly what I'd say next.

"Because you killed me!" I shouted. "If that doesn't mean you owe me one, I don't know what would."

Hades's face changed. Something flickered across his features, but it was too fast for me to read. His black eyes were filled with emotion, and the way he looked at me made me feel vulnerable all of a sudden.

Hades's magic flared, and as before, mine rose to answer, but my power was stronger than before. I was getting used to it, learning how to handle it, but the surge was unexpected, and our powers leaped toward each other. The moment it touched, the Earth shuddered.

My breath caught in my throat, and I struggled to keep my footing.

Hades looked surprised. "Elyse," he breathed.

The sound of his voice tugged at my core, and I was turned on. My body bloomed for him, heat spreading from the inside out. Hades's eyes filled with raw lust, but he shook his head and stepped away from me so that the link between our powers was severed.

"I'm going," he said again, then stormed away.

Shit. What was going on? I felt even less in control around the gods than I had been before with no idea how to cope with my attraction to him. Instead, I watched Hades leave, and a part of me yearned to call him back again. But I had pride. I wasn't going to run after the bastard who'd killed me, no matter how much I was still drawn to him. It was better to see Hades as the enemy, no matter what my emotions said.

My heart had gotten me into shit with this guy before. It was better that I learned from my mistakes than make them again.

Ares stepped up next to me. "What was that all about?"

"I can't explain it."

"The supernatural radar was off the chart. It sizzled over my skin."

I stared up at Ares, taking him in for the first time. He talked like he was in high school, but that was as far as the comparison went. Ares was tall and strong, muscles stacked wherever I looked. His hair was cut short against his scalp, and his green eyes were piercing. They were like gems staring out at me, and it was almost unnerving.

"Do you like what you see?" he asked.

I blushed immediately.

"You wish," I said. The truth was, I did like what I saw. "And where's your chariot? Heard you ride that everywhere you go." I cocked a brow, and he simply laughed.

Ares responded. "Zeus implied there's shit down here, and you need a sidekick."

"Stop making it sound like I'm the hero and you're the lowly minion," I said, remembering that Heracles was going to ask Zeus for help. But now that Ares stood there, all cocky and in my face, I wasn't a fan of having him as a sidekick.

"Yeah, you're right. Better let me be the hero." He flashed me a cocky grin with teeth that were impossibly white. "Where did you learn to fight like that?"

"Heracles," I responded.

Ares whistled through his teeth, his recently-shaven look adding to the whole "warrior look" he had going on, like he was ready for anything. He seemed the kind who would jump for the jugular when it came to battle... no holding back. He was the god of war, after all, though he wasn't a great team player from what I'd read about him. So how was this meant to work with him helping me?

"That's right," he said. "I heard he was babysitting now."

I rolled my eyes, grinding my teeth. "You should let him give you some pointers."

Ares laughed. "I'm the god of war, remember? I invented fighting."

"Maybe you're out of practice," I teased, smirking his way.

Ares cocked his eyebrow, clearly not impressed. "You're funny," he said. "It can't be Heracles's humor rubbing off on you."

I shook my head. "No, that's all my own."

Ares glanced around at the mess he'd made. The fallen trees, flattened benches. "Sorry about all this."

I sighed, glancing around too. The humans would attribute it to a small earthquake or something. Not that it was a likely thing to happen, but that was what they were going to do. People always needed to explain things.

"It's fine," I said.

"What's going on between you and Hades then?" Ares asked.

I gave him a sharp look. "Other than we're enemies?"

Ares laughed. "Sure, enemies always look like they want to bang."

"Who says *bang* anymore?" I asked.

Ares shook his head, still laughing. "You're changing the topic."

"And you're out of line," I replied. "That's twice in less than ten minutes. If you want to fight by my side, we need to work together. The point isn't for you to push me out of the way and do your own thing."

Ares pulled up his shoulders. "I've always done my own thing."

"Well, stop," I said. "I have to get out of here. I have things to do."

"Did I piss you off?" Ares asked.

I waved my hand in the air, dismissing him, convinced Zeus had made a mistake.

"Seriously," Ares said, and he came after me. I groaned. He grabbed my hand to stop me from walking away, but the moment our skins made contact, my power flared and searched for his.

Ares's power was violent, aggressive, wild. It didn't play nice with others. I could feel the defiance. But his power liked mine.

"This is unreal," Ares said, stepping closer to me. He wanted to explore what he was feeling. Maybe if I hadn't already reached my limit of magical connections for the past couple of days, I would have agreed.

The moment I thought about the whole linking thing, the desire intensified between us. Ares was hot in a reckless kind of way. His cocky smile, his arrogance, it reminded me of what it would be like to be free. I wanted a taste of that. I imagined my soul pressed up against his so I could feel what it was like not to be tethered to anything.

I broke the spell we were caught in and stepped away before I did anything stupid.

"Aw, buzzkill," Ares teased.

"Where did you learn to speak?" I asked.

Ares wiggled his eyebrows at me. "I knew you thought it was sexy."

I couldn't help but laugh. The humor was a relief from the sexual tension that had been building between us. I wanted the arrogant banter rather than another sexual attraction. I couldn't handle this right now. I needed to stay away from this kind of shit.

I had enough drama in my life with the two gods I was already falling for. To add a third would only drive me crazy.

"I have to go," I insisted.

"Cool. Where do you need me? When are we teaming up again?"

I shook my head. "I don't know. Go… wherever you go. Until I need you."

"You're dismissing me," Ares said, his eyes widening.

I nodded. I didn't know what else to say or how to make it sound polite.

But instead, he grinned at me, and even though he was acting weird, it was still a damn attractive smile. There was something light and easygoing about him, and after Hades and Apollo had been so damn intense, it was a welcome break.

But again, I couldn't deal with another man. Not now.

"I love it when the woman takes charge." Ares laughed, the sound teasing me.

"What?" I asked.

"Yeah. Tell me how to drive you crazy, and I'll do it. I'll take you to the stars, baby."

I couldn't keep from laughing.

"You're incorrigible," I said.

Ares shrugged, and even that was sexy. He didn't act like someone who was trying to be suave, but at the same time, he oozed sexuality.

Which meant Ares was as much trouble as the other two.

Was it going to be like this with all of them? I had no idea what to make of what I was feeling.

Multiple, in fact. Why were they all so interested in me?

For that matter, what drew me to them? Was I going god-crazy? Maybe spending too much time in their company had warped my mind, twisted my emotions.

I already knew the answer to that. It was our power. With Apollo, there was a lot more than just the magic. With Hades, there could have been. With Ares? He looked like he was always joking, but there was something there, deep inside. I could almost see it.

It made me want to dig for it, which was exactly why I had to get away from him.

"I'll see you around, my lady," Ares said.

I rolled my eyes, but before I could finish, Ares had vanished.

What the fuck was I going to do now?

Instead of heading home, I made my way to Heracles. He opened the door before I knocked.

"I was waiting for you to come cry on my shoulder," Heracles joked. "I already made coffee."

I didn't respond to his jokes. "Zeus sent Ares," I blurted out.

"What?" His mouth dropped open, his nose scrunched up.

I nodded. "Yeah, that's what I said."

Heracles shook his head and let me into the house.

"That doesn't make sense. What good is he going to do?"

I shrugged. "I don't know. He fucked up my fight with Hades today."

Heracles stilled. "You fought Hades again?"

I nodded. "The asshole still acts like it's fine that he killed me."

Heracles only glared at me.

"What?" I asked, not needing his judgment right now. Or ever. I barely understood what was happening to me, why I longed for Apollo to be with me twenty-four-seven, why thinking of Hades burned me up from the inside out. So I did the only thing possible…pushed them away to let my brain catch up. To sort out my shit. Then I'd take it slow with Apollo.

He shook his head. "Nothing."

We strolled into the kitchen, where the smell of coffee hung thick in the air.

"Tell me what the god of *waste of my time* did," Heracles said.

They all had nicknames for him, I noticed. Ares wasn't a favorite among the gods. I had read about that once, but seeing it firsthand was different.

I started telling Heracles what had happened, how Ares had arrived, and what he'd done. I explained how the fight had been interrupted and then ended.

What I didn't add was that despite how corny and quirky Ares was, there was something about him that was sexy as hell. I didn't add how my power was attracted to his power, and I didn't mention that sending Ares away had been for me more than for him. Because I couldn't deny I was attracted to Ares. And that scared me.

I refused to do something with yet another god because my power demanded it and because there was something deep down inside that I couldn't see yet. Something I wanted to find. Something I knew I could fall for.

But right now I tried to sort through my emotions to make things work with Apollo and me because he touched me, affected me, loved me in a way that called to me. And in my mind, he was mine, but I just had to get my shit together for once.

And why did I always see this in the gods? Why was there always something I yearned to make my own with them?

I was only going to get myself in trouble if I carried on like this. It wasn't like things were particularly easy as it was. I had to keep myself in check. I had to be sure I didn't let anything happen with Ares. There was no reason to turn the god of war into my personal god of love too.

CHAPTER 25

Elyse

*C*raziest week ever! I collapsed onto my bed, face-first, and lay there, my body aching all over. My life felt like a whirlwind from battling gods, falling for them, still needing to defeat X, oh, and I'd died. Now Zeus had sent Ares as my sidekick. What was he thinking? Like I needed more men and complication in my life.

A knock came at my door, and I propped my head up, staring at the clock on my bedside stand. Ten o'clock at night, and in all honesty, I had no idea who it could be, though I had planned on a long shower followed by devouring some coconut sorbet.

I climbed off the bed, dragged myself to the door, and opened it. In the doorway stood Apollo, wearing the widest grin, one hand pressed up against the frame, the other in the pocket of his jeans. His sexy eyes sparkled, and the energy within me surged forward, engulfing me, owning me, demanding I take what was mine.

"What are you doing here?" I teased.

He didn't say a word but strolled inside, so I shut the door behind him.

"I want alone time with you. No interruptions, no other gods, or anything else. Just you and me."

He took my arm, drawing me against him. The touch ignited my fire further, burning deep between my legs. His hands sailed to my face, cupping my cheeks, and he kissed me without a word. His scorching lips melted me, and I softened against him. The hunger in his kiss drew me closer. Our chests pressed together, the inferno between us intensifying.

"I couldn't stay away," he breathed against my mouth. "I want you so much, no matter the consequences."

Stiffening, I looked into the bluest eyes. "What consequences?"

He kissed me again, my thoughts stolen, every worry in the world fading. "I wanted to take you on a small getaway tonight," he said, his arms still looped around me tightly.

"What do you have in mind?" Curiosity threaded through me because it was a nice change to have someone come to my door with a promise of fun instead of doom and gloom. We stared at each other, both desire and hunger glowing in his gaze.

"You'll see, sweetheart." When his mouth pressed against mine, the world around me disappeared, and I drowned in his emotions. A tingling sensation prickled my flesh, and there was nowhere else I'd long to be but in Apollo's arms. He affected me like no other. I craved him, needed him. His insistent mouth was parting my lips, and I was dissolving into his love, forgetting everything but the two of us.

A cold breeze blew across my nape, icy claws digging into my flesh. Panic struck my chest. Was X back? I broke free from Apollo's embrace, glancing around to a world cloaked in night.

I was no longer in my apartment, or Chicago for that

matter. The wind whistled in my ears and darkness encased us. I rubbed my eyes to settle in with the scene as a bitter chill settled in my bones. The moon's silver glow lit up the wooden platform we stood on, encased by a railing. We were on the side of a mountain so damn high up in the air. All I could see were enormous shadows towering around us like gods... But they were mountains, so many of them, the snow coating them glistening in the moonlight.

I wore a fur coat that fell to my feet, keeping some of the cold at bay, but my fingers were icy cold.

"W-Where are we?"

I turned to Apollo, who was also bundled up. He took my hand and cupped it in his, warming me in seconds, the heat sliding up my arm and whisking through me.

The silvery moonlight illuminated the side of his gorgeous face. His blue eyes pierced through the night—and his lips stretched wide, as if proud of his surprise. I wasn't so sure yet.

"Did you know that Mont Blanc is the highest mountain in the French Alps?" He glanced over to an oversized range towering in the distance.

"We're in France?" Okay, I hadn't traveled much, let alone visit Europe. I gasped and leaned against the railing, staring out into the night, then hurried along the length of the platform, bouncing on my toes. At our backs sat a building, windows dark, and I could only imagine this place was a lookout for tourists, or even a research location. But who the hell cared? I was in freaking France!

Except I wished it were daytime so I could see the splendor. Then again, I was dating a god and we could return anytime, right? So were we officially dating? Was that what I called falling for the god of the sun?

Apollo closed in behind me and locked his arms around my stomach, holding me tight and close. "I brought you here to be as high as possible, and where the moon is so full that it feels like you could almost touch it. And I wanted you to see its beauty."

I leaned back into his embrace and stared up at the great luminous moon, its light pouring from the heavens across the land. It was enormous, and Apollo was right: the longer I looked at the moon, the closer it appeared to be easily within arm's reach. Silver sequins blinked in the heavens, scattered, illuminating the sky. I could stargaze for eternity, admiring the cluster of galaxies, making everything else feel so insignificant. Was this how the gods felt looking down on Earth?

"Wow! It's incredible up here." My breath formed a mist that floated in front of my face.

Apollo spun me around by my shoulders to face him, and he pulled open his coat, drawing me into his warmth. "For you, I'd capture the moon in the sky."

And I believed him. My frozen lips found his warm ones as my breath hitched at his words. I drank in his passion, our bodies pressed tight, his hardness nestled against my stomach. Didn't matter where we were, that magnetic attraction between us blossomed. His presence fogged my mind, and my body tingled to have him take me. I ran my fingers up his neck, adoring everything about Apollo.

"I don't plan to let you go," he said, "and I'll do whatever it takes to ensure we stay together."

The fire flickered in his eyes and the honesty of his voice touched me because he clearly meant every word, and I couldn't deny how much he meant to me.

"I haven't been able to stop thinking about you," I said. "I miss you when you're not around. But I worry about X and the other gods and how that will impact us. I *will* fight X, you know that? And I can't have you standing in my way."

"Shhh…now is not the time for such things. It's just you and me tonight, remember?"

He was right. Enjoy the moment, I mean I freaking died. And after everything I'd been through I knew that moments like this were precious and fleeting. I swallowed past the lump wedged in my throat.

Of course he was right, but it wasn't that simple. Nothing ever was. That bastard X had affected me, drawn out my anger to make me fight when I should've used my head. But I refused to get into an argument about that now. X had ruined enough, and tonight was about Apollo and me.

"The future isn't always what we think it will be," he added. "What we can control is today." He dug a hand into his pocket and opened his curled fingers.

In his palm sat a golden chain with a round glass ball. White sand—or was it snow?—half-filled the pendant.

"I have a small gift for you," he said. "And it shines like the moon."

My mouth opened, but no words came out because the last person who'd given me a present had been my dad. He'd offered me his set of daggers that my grandfather had presented to him. A family heirloom. But Apollo's surprise was different. This came from his heart, and with the love in his eyes when he studied me, I was lost.

"It's stunning." I reached out to the chain tenderly, lifting it out of his hand, studying the fine particles in the ball, the way the contents glinted in the dark. "Are they powdered moon rocks?"

"It's the essence from within the moon, and it will always brighten the way for you when I'm not around. Let me put it on."

He collected the necklace from my hand, and I turned away from him, lifting my braid away from my neck. Once his gift was clasped around my neck, I faced Apollo once more, fingering my pendant, staring down as it sat in the center of my chest, gleaming with a silvery hue.

"It's beautiful. I love it so much." I glanced up at him, my throat closing up with emotion at the mesmerizing gift.

"I'd give you anything to keep you smiling. I want to show you the world, its splendor, the good that Earth has to offer."

His words fluttered through me because I had fallen for a man... no, a *god* who offered me the world and I had no doubt he meant every word.

"I want to make this work," I said, pressing against his chest, his arms wrapping around my back.

"We will." He kissed the top of my head and we stayed there for what felt like eternity. I was embraced by a god while I stared out at the heavens of the gods.

A cold breeze rushed past, raising the hairs on my arms, and Apollo held me tighter. "Let's head inside. The sun will rise in two hours and I want you to see its beauty. It will be glorious this morning."

How could it not be when the god of the sun promised it would?

He leaned down, one arm under my knees, the other at my back, and lifted me into his arms with such swiftness, I lost my breath.

"Tonight, you're mine. Plus, I've arranged some of the finest cheeses and wines France has to offer." He winked and I snuggled against his chest, unable to believe I could feel such ecstasy and joy after the week I'd had. But from my first time with Apollo, I'd known he affected me like no other. We'd bonded before I'd understood what was going on. And this was so much deeper than our sexual arousal—it was something I needed to explore further, as if my life depended on it. To finally give myself permission to date someone, not fear they wouldn't understand about my missions. Apollo was part of my world and if anyone would be there when I needed support, he would be the one to catch me when I fell.

The fight with Hades swooped into my mind in that very moment, and how Apollo had not taken my side, but hell, I knew why he hadn't jumped in and that he had kept X at bay. It still sat heavily on my chest, especially with Hades's approach to stopping me. But I hadn't exactly been acting rational, either. And trying to work it out hurt my head, so I shoved those thoughts aside. I wouldn't let them ruin the best night of my life.

I was with Apollo in the French Alps, and he'd gifted me a piece of the freaking moon. Nothing else compared. Not a single thing.

Oh, except knowing Apollo, the god of the sun, was all mine!

CHAPTER 26

Elyse

*W*hen I woke up in bed, something felt wrong. But it shouldn't have been. Not after I'd spent half the night in the French Alps with Apollo. After a couple of hours of scorching hot sex, we had watched the glorious sunrise in each other's arms. A moment I'd never forget. After he had brought me back home, I crashed from exhaustion once he left.

But right now, it was still dark outside. Chicago remained asleep, and the city's silence engulfed me. I snuggled back under the covers, about to drift off to sleep when the hairs on my arms lifted, followed by waves of magic pulsating through the air, crackling over my skin.

The moment it tingled on my flesh, I jolted up in bed and rubbed my eyes. "What the hell now?"

Was this never going to end? I desired one night where I could sleep without getting interrupted by this shit. One day where I could focus on training without needing to fight. Better yet, a day off. I glanced over at my nightstand, at the necklace with the moon's essence that Apollo had gifted me, my insides beaming. Maybe I'd spend today with him by the beach or whatever a normal woman did with a new man in her life. Plus, I'd been battling since last week and deserved time off.

But as the power built around me, bubbling, heating me, I knew I wasn't going to be able to ignore this. Whatever it was, whoever was doing this, it would turn into another fight. I could almost feel the burning energy scoring my skin.

I climbed out of bed and dragged on my fighting clothes, as if this had become the status quo. If I was going to be drawn into battle, I wasn't going to do it in my pajamas. I had my limitations.

When I stepped outside the apartment, dawn hung low like fog. In the middle of the vortex of power stood Hades on my sidewalk, his shoulders slightly hunched and his mouth drawn into a hard line. My insides hummed.

"What are you doing here?" I demanded, exhaustion pushing through me. I realized I should have recognized the magic that had woken me up, but it had caught me off-guard.

"I want to talk to you," Hades said, his voice low and calm.

"So you called me with your power?" Except, I didn't care. I shook my head, not interested in hearing what he had to say. If he needed to do anything, we could fight, finish what we started. And I was stronger now and was about to tell him so when I took a good look at him.

His clothes hung from his frame, as if he had lost weight, although his physique was still spectacular. Hades had lean muscles, unlike those of Apollo or Ares. He appeared more regal. But his handsome face was tired, his eyes weary, and he didn't have his pitchfork with him. Though he could pull it from nothing like he had last time.

"About what?" I asked, instead of telling him to fuck off or fighting him.

"Your death."

I groaned. "What is it you want to tell me, that you're sorry? I guess this is the only case in which your work can be undone when you actually kill someone. Because I came back to life."

"I didn't want to do it," Hades pleaded. "Please believe me. But you wouldn't stop, and losing you wasn't an option."

"Sure you didn't." I folded my arms over my chest. I knew what I had felt for him when we'd been together, but I couldn't trust him. There had to have been other options than killing me.

"You were going to fight X. He was going to murder you. It was the only way to stop you, and I couldn't lose you," he murmured, a tremble underlining his words.

Silence filled the air between us, but inside my head, the pounding of my heart continued.

I shook my head, my throat thickening, and my fingers tingled for him, so I curled them. "Don't tell me there was no other way."

Hades just stared at me, and it made me think back to that night. I had been forcing away the memories of that incident, but this time, I allowed myself to think back properly.

I had fought with vigor that night. I had managed to reach down deep and find power I hadn't even known I was capable of releasing. It had been a hell of a battle, and I'd had every intention to get past Hades and confront X himself. That asshole had killed innocents.

He probably would have killed me, and if I'd had my head screwed on right, I would have stopped.

"So you killed me so X wouldn't?" I asked, gripping my hips.

Hades nodded. "You have no idea what that decision did to me."

I remained skeptical there wasn't another option. "You're right, I don't. Tell me."

Hades inhaled deeply. "What I feel for you is a hell of a lot more than I should be feeling for anyone. I'm not going to lie about it. I won't admit it when anyone asks, but I care for you. Killing you damn near ripped my heart out."

When he said it, his emotions were raw, touching me when they shouldn't have.

"You couldn't have knocked me out instead?" I asked. "Killing me was a dick move if you really cared."

"You wouldn't have stopped," he snarled.

I stared down at my curled hands, then back up at him. The reason this pissed me off so much was because I did care for Hades. "You could have chained me up or something, but when you..." I didn't want to keep saying the words. So much had gone wrong that night, and I wasn't sure whom I ought to have been more pissed off at. Hades for killing me, at myself for not being strong enough to withstand X's influence, or X. Okay, X was up there, the asshole, but I'd never expected Hades to hurt me.

"You proved to me you were evil by doing exactly the one thing good guys don't do."

"I chose the lesser of two evils," Hades said, his chin lifting.

Our voices were raised, as was the tension in the air. But I liked fighting him in a way. Hades was a good opponent, and engaging him gave me an outlet for my pent-up emotions.

I much rather preferred other things with him, though. I shouldn't have thought about it. The moment I did, arousal flared up, and my power surged forward. Hades stepped closer, as if he were being drawn to me like a magnet.

"I can taste your magic," he said in a whisper. "It's so strong. So fucking strong I can't think of anything else."

I nodded, swallowing hard. The problem was, the more

potent my magic became, the more power it called from the gods. Hades's energy wrapped around me, and it was cool on my skin, the promise of secrets and danger lurking beneath the surface. It was delicious. The danger, the darkness, was attractive. With Hades, I toyed with seeing how far we could push it. To find where the edge was and how far we could shuffle before we tumbled off.

Hades closed the distance between us in a second and pressed his lips against mine. It was unexpected, but I had ached for the feel of his mouth on mine. His energy slithered over my skin, cold and wet like a snake, and my power accommodated it, responding in the same strange manner. This was new. My ability had changed, and I was still getting to know the power. The sexual need inside me had become overwhelming, burning me, shoving aside all rationality. I had to have Hades. My apartment was right here. In the back of my mind, I thought of Apollo, but it wasn't as simple as belonging to a single god. I felt that now, just as Heracles had tried to explain.

It was never that simple with them, and I got it now. Except I wasn't ready to just jump back into his arms, as much as every molecule in my body insisted. I stepped back from him. I needed my head straight.

"We should get some breakfast perhaps," he suggested. He must have sensed me pulling away, though his ravenous gaze was anything but calm. His eyes drowned in desire, but the shit between Hades and me wasn't over. And I wanted to talk about things.

"There's a small café open a few blocks away," I said.

Hades nodded. "Let's go."

I took his hand to lead him away from my apartment, but he pulled me against him. The length of his body was pressed up to mine, and I felt his erection, long and hard against my pelvis and lower stomach. He wanted this—needed this—as much as I craved our time together.

"No," I said. "I still haven't forgiven you."

The Earth started to tremble beneath my feet. Hades had his arms wrapped around me, tightening as if nothing would dare pry me from his grasp.

"What are you doing to the ground?" I asked.

"I'm not doing anything." He glanced up and down the empty sidewalk in front of the apartment.

Raindrops fell from the sky, first one by one, slowly picking up to become more and more. We both looked up. The water fell down in a sheet that was so solid, it was almost like a bucket had been upended and the water was rushing to Earth.

"Oh, no," Hades said.

"What's going on?"

He pinched the bridge of his nose. "I'm so sick of this shit."

I frowned, opening my mouth to ask, but the heavens opened and a god stepped down from the heavens.

He was older, with long, black hair that hung in curls on his shoulders and a distinguished face, angular and handsome. His eyes were the color of the ocean, a deep blue that went on forever, and he stood with an authority that would have driven fear into the hearts of men.

But I wasn't just any human. Hades looked irritated if anything, his brow pinched, lips twisted into a wry frown.

"You couldn't stay away, could you?" Hades cried out.

I shook my head. Who the hell was this?

The stranger strode toward us, and the power rolled off him in waves, making me feel like I couldn't breathe, as if I were submerged in water.

"You can't stay out of trouble for one century, can you?" the new god asked.

Hades groaned. "I don't need you here."

"The presence of X says otherwise," his voice boomed.

"I'm sorry to interrupt, but who are you?" I asked as he strode toward us up the sidewalk.

Hades sighed.

"You don't recognize me?" the new god asked, a brow arched.

"It's my brother," Hades growled.

I looked at the god again, and suddenly, I could see it. I smelled the ocean, tasted the salt on my tongue. My skin was damp with the sea breeze, and I breathed in deeply. The strangest sensations accompanied it. A feeling of being... home, which I didn't understand.

"Poseidon," I breathed.

ABOUT MILA YOUNG

Bestselling author, Mila Young tackles everything with the zeal and bravado of the fairytale heroes she grew up reading about. She slays monsters, real and imaginary, like there's no tomorrow. By day she rocks a keyboard as a marketing extraordinaire. At night she battles with her might pen-sword, creating fairytale retellings, and sexy ever after tales. In her spare time, she loves pretending she's a mighty warrior, walks on the beach with her dogs, cuddling up with her cats, and devouring every fantasy tale she can get her pinkies on.

Ready for the next story from Mila Young? Subscribe today: www.subscribepage.com/milayoung

Mila Young loves to connect with readers.
For more information...
milayoungauthor@gmail.com
www.facebook.com/milayoungauthor
twitter.com/MilaYoungAuthor